MEMOIRS
of a
COSSACK
WARRIOR

D.W. Roth

Memoirs Of A Cossack Warrior
Copyright © 2022 by D.W. Roth

ISBN: Paperback: 978-1-63945-027-5
       Hardcover: 978-1-63945-029-9

All rights reserved. No part of this publication may be reproduced, distributed, or transmitted in any form or by any means, including photocopying, recording, or other electronic or mechanical methods, without the prior written permission of the publisher, except in the case brief quotations embodied in critical reviews and other noncommercial uses permitted by copyright law.

The views expressed in this book are solely those of the author and do not necessarily reflect the views of the publisher, and the publisher hereby disclaims any responsibility for them.

Writers' Branding 1 800-608-6550
www.writersbranding.com
orders@writersbranding.com

Contents

DEDICATION vii
ACKNOWLEDGEMENTS ix
PREFACE xi

CHAPTER I 1
    INTRODUCTION TO WAR 1
    INTRODUCTION TO THE ROTH FAMILY 2
    AUTHOR 4
    LAMBER T 4
    THE ROTH FAMILY DEPARTS FOR RUSSIA 4
    ARRIVAL IN ODESSA 11

CHAPTER II 13
    BACK TO REALITY 13
    HISTORY OF NICHOLAS II 15
    ANASTASIA'S DESTINY 18

CHAPTER III 21
    DAD BUILDS A NEW HOUSE 21
    THE CZAR'S CHOSEN FEW 24
    XAVIER, MISSING IN ACTION 32
    XAVIER'S STORY 33

CHAPTER IV 37
    MEMORIES 37
    LAMBERT MEETS MAGGI 38

CHAPTER V 45
    WEDDING 45
    CEREMONY 46
    RECEPTION 46

CHAPTER VI 57
    CEASEFIRE 57
    PEACE TALKS 58

CHAPTER VII 59
    MICHAEL CAPTURED 59
    MICHAEL MEETS SONJA 61

SONJA'S STORY 64
CHAPTER VIII 73
    XAVIER, ALIAS FATHER JAMES 73
    XAVIER IMPRISONED BY IVAN 74
    XAVIER AND IVAN MAKE PEACE 78
CHAPTER IX 81
    ANNA'S HOUSE FIRE 81
    BON VOYAGE TO MOM AND DAD 82
    XAVIER 88
    ANNA'S STORY 90
    WEDDING 93
CHAPTER X 95
    MICHAEL'S SEARCH FOR SONJA 95
    MICHAEL MEETS A NEW FRIEND 98
    MICHAEL'S INFATUATION 100
    MICHAEL'S STORY 102
    MICHAEL FINDS SONJA 103
CHAPTER XI 105
    FUTURE PLANS 105
    DEPART FOR SPAIN 108
    ISABELLA KIDNAPPED 109
    RESCUE OF ISABELLA 117
    XAVIER'S DEPARTURE FOR AMERICA 122
CHAPTER XII 125
    TRAVEL TO MADRID 125
    SPANISH WEDDING TO PRINCES ISABELLA 128
    NEW HACIENDA 131
CHAPTER XIII 137
    ARRIVING IN SOUTH DAKOTA 137
    TORNADO 138
CHAPTER XIV 141
    DAD COLLAPSES 141
    FINDING DAD'S OLD LOVE LETTERS 142
    SEARCHING FOR OUR LOST BROTHER JAMES 143

CHAPTER XV 147
    LOCATED LOST BROTHER JAMES 147
    CORRESPONDING WITH JAMES 149
CHAPTER XVI 157
    JAMES VISITS SOUTH DAKOTA 157
    BONDING WITH JAMES 160
    GETTING ACQUAINTED 162
    FREDRICK REMINISCING 163
CHAPTER XVII 167
    VISITING JAMES IN MINNEAPOLIS 167
CHAPTER XVIII 171
    MICHAEL INVITES MOM TO VISIT SPAIN 171
    DINNER WITH THE KING 176
    MOM'S VISIT TO SPAIN 176
CHAPTER XIX 183
    BROTHERS INVITED TO SPAIN 183
CHAPTER XX 187
    BROTHERS VISIT SPAIN 187
    BROTHERS CONFRONT PIRATES 188
    BROTHERS REWARDED BY KING 190
CHAPTER XXI 193
    BROTHERS RETURN HOME 193
    JAMES MEETS MICHAEL 194
CHAPTER XXII 197
    SONJA'S STOPOVER IN VALENCIA 197
    SONJA DINES WITH MICHAEL 200
CHAPTER XXIII 203
    SERENDIPITY 203

EPILOGUE 205
AUTHOR'S NOTES 207
SELECT BIBLIOGRAPHY 209
PERSONAL INTERVIEWS 211

DEDICATION

This story, for the most part, is based on facts. It depicts how these three brothers were able to survive "The Living Hell" and return from those horrendous, life-threatening battles to pursue a somewhat normal life of happiness. Their faith and strong upbringing gave these three brothers the inward strength and tenacity necessary to endure these many turns of events that were their outrageous misfortune to bear. These stories of war, love, and compassion are certain to move even the most discerning reader.

ACKNOWLEDGEMENTS

I wish to express my sincere thanks to my son, Douglas Roth, a great- grandson of Lambert, for his tireless efforts in transcribing this entire biography from its original handwritten format to the present high- tech, computerized product. Without his expertise, this task would have grieved me considerably.

—Dad

PREFACE

In the decades leading up to the Bolshevik Revolution and the Great War, when revolt was widespread and the value of life was diminishing rapidly, the crowned heads of Europe were frantically struggling to maintain power over the populace. These power struggles came at a high cost of human lives as these madmen dictators used their citizens as pawns in their bloody war games.

Around the year 1890, the Roth family was compelled to move to Russia from their home in Wiesbaden, Germany, to avoid the revolution that was threatening their homeland. They were not aware that Russia too was experiencing political unrest. Unfortunately, they soon found themselves, once again, in harm's way.

In order to support his military might, Czar Nicholas II founded the Russian Cossacks, as they came to be known. Unlike the previous ethnic Cossacks, these Cossacks were intrepid giants who rode swift horses and yielded to no man. They were feared by all and rightfully so. They mostly hailed from regions outside of Russia; thus, they were not predominately Russian citizens. Most were conscripted or forced at gunpoint to fight for the czar, including thousands of disgruntled German immigrants who protested violently. Among those were my grandfather, Lambert Roth, and his two brothers, Xavier and Michael, all near giants—each one exceeding six-foot-six-inches tall. They had never in their adult lives experienced fear or defeat. However, they were kidnapped by the Russian Military Command and forced into service as Cossack Warriors.

After their release from service to the czar, the brothers still found themselves in a dangerous world. They faced many perils, searching to find the women whom they loved amongst the rubble of Russian civilization. Along with their parents, they immigrated to the United States or Spain and set up new homes once again, where their adventures continued for several more years.

AUTHOR *****

By the age of sixteen, my writing skills had caught the eye of several accomplished writers of fine literature. My grandfather, Lambert Roth, approached me one day and asked if I would like to help him write a book from his memoirs.

"That's a great idea," I responded. "If you can get your memoirs translated into English, I think we can get started."

I only spoke a few words of German, so I needed Grandfather and a good translator to accomplish this difficult task. Interruptions seemed to plague our efforts. Time was difficult to find, but eventually I managed to finish writing my outline on the major issues of this story.

Now, after many years and many incomplete attempts, I have kept my word and have finally finished this biography. My grandfather has since passed on, but I feel that he would be as proud of our joint effort as I am.

The following is the essence of his story, along with many other extraordinary events that continue to capture my imagination even today. More than 115 years have passed since my grandfather and his brothers' experiences in the Cossacks, but these fascinating stories remain as written in their memoirs and as told to me in stages when I was just a boy.

Although fictional in certain places to enable me to connect the dots and maintain continuity, the vast majority of this story is incredibly true.

Some names and places are fictional; however, after tireless research, most remain factual. Some of the dates quoted herein are approximate while others may vary only slightly from the actual recorded historic dates.

With much honor and great pride, I humbly submit the stories and experiences of those fearless, giant warriors who survived "The Living Hell." These men were my ancestors, the seed of my seed. Although sworn duty compels me to share these incredible stories from my grandfather and his two brothers, I feel honored to immortalize these brave warriors with their own remarkable stories:

a. Simon and Ingrid Roth, parents of Xavier, Lambert, and Michael
b. Xavier Roth and Anna his wife
c. Lambert Roth (my grandfather) and Maggi (my adorable Irish grandmother) his wife
d. Michael Roth and Isabella, his wife and Spanish princess
e. Sonja, a nun who was once engaged to Michael
e. James Roth (half-brother to Lambert, Xavier, and Michael) and Kathleen, his wife
f. Ejon Vogel of the Swiss Underground, who helped displaced people from various conflicts in the late 1800s and the early 1900s
g. D. W. Roth the author and grandson of Lambert

*Note: Because these memoirs were initially written in the first person, the speaker changes throughout the narrative to reflect the source material.

CHAPTER I
LAMBERT
INTRODUCTION TO WAR

We were trained to "kill or be killed." The Cossacks were all sizable men who rode fast horses, giving us a huge advantage over our enemy. As we charged through their ranks, we were chopping, slicing, and impaling all those who dared challenge us. Our foot soldiers followed close behind, finishing off the Opposition.

The first night after battle, as I rode through the field of dead warriors, I told myself, *War is Hell*. This wanton slaughter of mankind was driven by the strongest instinct known to man, survival, which contributed vastly to the senseless killings of our so-called enemy as well as thousands of our own warriors. These young men were not my enemies, but it was them or us as was our constant reminder.

I was exhausted, and my mind was racing as I recalled the horrific events of the day. How I managed to survive such an ordeal was incomprehensible to me, and as I fell asleep, I drifted back to the days of my youth, in Germany.

INTRODUCTION TO THE ROTH FAMILY

I was in town showing my prize bull at a national competition. We had won the Grand Championship trophy that day and a $1,500 cash prize for first place.

While waiting for Dad to pick me up, four men suddenly attacked me. They tied me with ropes, beat me severely, and stole my money. The champion bull turned up missing, and I was extremely worried.

Dad soon came to my rescue, but the robbers were nowhere to be found. After searching for over an hour, we located my bull in a nearby barn; fortunately, he was unharmed. We enlisted the help of the local sheriff, who instantly staked out the area. It wasn't long before a group of drunken cowboys returned to the barn and were immediately taken into custody by the sheriff. The culprits were headed for jail, and my remaining prize money, a mere $1,242 was quickly returned to me.

We hurried home to find the rest of the family, Mom, Xavier, and Michael, just finishing dinner. Dad soon began giving a report on the homestead land in Russia, from where he had just returned. This land was on the Black Sea and was free to German immigrant farmers who wanted to homestead some fine farmland. The homesteads were being offered by the Russian government to grow crops for its starving citizens. "It's ours for the taking," Dad remarked. "All we need to do is sign our names, and once we have lived on the land for five years, the land is ours.

Xavier asked, "What did it look like, Dad?

"The soil is black and sandy and full of nutrients, and the weather is like summer all year 'round. There's plenty of water for crops, and the pasture is tall and green. It is the best farmland that I've ever seen."

"The word on the street here in Germany is that a revolution is impending," Dad continued.

"I'm afraid that you boys will be called to fight before we can sell out and leave."

Ingrid asked, "How soon do you think it will start, Simon? "I wish I knew, but it looks like any day now."

"Yes, Dad, let's go," Xavier added. "Let's sell everything and get out while we can."

He didn't like the thought of war or the thought of killing. He was a Christian and had been studying for the priesthood. He didn't know anything about war and didn't care to learn as he was a farmer, not a military man.

Dad suggested, "Why take a chance? Let's go now, or we may regret it. I think it's best that we get started early in the morning as it will take a few days to liquidate everything."

"What about your seminary studies, Xavier? I don't think you'll be able to continue in Russia as I believe they only have Russian Orthodox there."

"That's okay, Dad, I'll address that after we've moved on. The important thing is that we avoid this impending revolution."

"I'm sorry it worked out this way, son, but you will be able to finish your studies once this is all over."

Xavier replied, "I agree, let's continue with our plans and leave right away. We can sell the livestock to Mr. Goring at the cattle exchange as he's always looking to buy more cattle."

Dad warned, "We don't dare tell anyone else our plans as we must be very careful. My brother, Nick, has asked to buy our home and our land. He has no sons to worry about for the war and has offered to pay off our loan and give us over $10,000 cash. What do you think, Ingrid?" "I say yes, Simon. Let's sell it to him and go quickly before the fighting begins."

AUTHOR

Everyone agreed to this plan, so they began implementing it at dawn. Simon sold almost everything except a team of horses and a large wagon filled with their personal belongings. He also kept his old saddle horse, Blackie, which he planned to ride all the way to Odessa.

LAMBER T
THE ROTH FAMILY DEPARTS FOR RUSSIA

We departed for Russia in four days and not one day too soon. We saw many soldiers marching along the roadway as they prepared for the revolution, but we attracted no attention.

Our wagon was loaded for the trip with everything we hadn't sold. We knew it would be a long, tiring trip as we would need to rest our horses every few hours. Dad had just traveled this road when he went to look at the homestead land four weeks earlier; this was a big advantage to us now.

We were very cautious as we departed Wiesbaden, trying not to attract attention and praying that all would go well. Xavier and I were out of sight, riding inside the wagon for fear the revolutionaries might take us to fight. Mom and Fritz, our dog, rode on the seat beside Michael, who was driving the team.

Dad rode ahead at first, always alert, and trying to avoid any possibility of trouble. He didn't expect to find any, but he felt better scouting ahead of the wagon for now.

After we had been on the road for a while, we stopped to water our horses and discovered about fifty riders with rifles who had gathered there. They appeared to be revolutionaries looking for recruits. Dad spotted them immediately, and to avoid any problems, he told Xavier and me to remain inside the wagon.

The soldiers talked to Mom and Michael, but they could see that Michael was just a teenager. Mom told them that we were moving to Dresden, near the border.

They warned her to look out for fighting along the border as countless refugees were trying to cross into Russia, without visas.

Each day we traveled, we could feel the climate change. Odessa was a resort area and was much warmer than Wiesbaden; we welcomed the glowing sun. We also knew that the farming would be much better in this climate, and the profits from our crops would probably double, particularly with water available for irrigation.

We had been warned about the robbers on the road, who would come along during the night and rob travelers. Dad was always on the alert for such highway robbers. He made a special box and bolted it out of sight to the frame of the wagon. He then put a chain around it and locked it to keep our valuables safe.

Dad always rode Blackie and stayed close to the wagon so that he could watch for trouble. He carried both a pistol and a rifle with him, and we had a rifle aboard the wagon as well. We tried to take extra precautions so as not to be vulnerable.

On the third day from home, we noticed two tacky-looking tramps hanging around us. That night, while we were sleeping, Fritz started barking and awakened us. We could see some people going through our wagon, so Dad drew his pistol and fired a shot over their heads; they quickly scattered in the dark. The next morning, Dad checked everything and said that there was nothing missing from the wagon.

We continued along this roadway and were very careful after that because we had our entire fortune with us. Dad and Xavier wore their pistols on their belts to scare off any robbers, while the rifle remained in plain view beside the driver on the wagon; now we felt safe.

Each night, we tried to camp where there were other wagons and people. Fritz was always bedded down by the front axle to alert us in case of intruders. One night, however, we were far from any campground, and it began to get dark. We had stopped to make a repair on our brakes, but we were unable to catch the other wagons that had been traveling with us.

Mom felt uneasy camping alone, but we had no choice. Dad built a big fire, and each of us boys took a two-hour watch during the night. All went well until about two o'clock when Michael fell asleep on watch. I heard a big commotion, and the dog started barking aggressively.

Then four masked men, all holding pistols, rushed us. The dog continued barking until one of the robbers shot him. He yelped painfully and ran off in the dark.

They tied us all together and helped themselves to some food and coffee. They took Dad's Gold pocket watch and demanded our money, which remained well protected in Dad's lockbox and out of site.

We were still tied with the ropes when the sun came up, but once we could see, we were able to free ourselves. We learned a good lesson that night, and that was never camp alone.

As we were eating breakfast, Fritz came limping up on three legs, so we bandaged his paw and fed him. He seemed to be doing much better and rode the rest of the way beside Mom in the wagon.

Dad rode ahead to find a campsite, and we gladly spent the night with a large group of travelers. We needed fresh water, so we filled every jug we had with good springwater before leaving camp. We were happy just to be safe and back on the road once again.

We had to cross a mountain pass that day, so we took some time to check everything before we left camp, particularly our brakes. Others saw us doing this and asked Dad if we had a problem.

"No," he said.

"I'm only checking everything to make sure we don't have a problem in the mountains."

We had never been in the mountains before and didn't know what to expect. We asked travelers, who were coming from the other direction about the road conditions. They said to be extremely careful and stay out of the ruts. We were very apprehensive and afraid of the unknown, so we traveled slowly and stayed with the other wagons to avoid any chance of a problem.

It had been raining, and the road was already cut up with deep ruts and holes in the mud. Other travelers were stuck up to their axles, but we couldn't stop to help them for fear we would never get through ourselves. There were two local guys, with some large workhorses, helping people get their wagons out of the mud holes. I'm sure that those locals charged plenty of money for their help.

We had passed the worst section of road, but nightfall came before we got off the mountain. We had become desperate to find a campground, and finally we came upon a meadow where others were camping for the night. Our horses were tired from the hard pull up the hill, and there was plenty of grass for pasture. Not forgetting our night of camping alone, we quickly decided to make camp.

There were many friendly folks quite like ourselves and far from home, who were traveling to a new land where people and customs were much different and endless opportunities abounded. We visited with other travelers and traded stories of the trip thus far.

One man with a wife and three little girls told of being robbed recently. They had been camping alone at night. He said there were only two armed men, but he didn't have a gun to protect himself and his family. Dad invited him to travel with us, and we all pitched in to help them buy some food and supplies so they could reach their destination. As we continued on our journey, we discovered many nice people traveling to Odessa. We traded stories, shared our thoughts, and just visited, reassuring each other of the safety in numbers. Dad was always happy to make new friends as we sat around the fire at night making plans for the next day. Mom would usually ask how each of us was doing, and then she would tell us how wonderful life was going to be on the Black Sea.

Each day took a little more out of us, and we still had eight more days travel to Odessa. One late afternoon, we had to ford a river. As soon as we got across, we set up camp along with many others.

Dad yelled out, "It's time for a bath, everyone!"

We all grabbed a bar of soap before we jumped into the river and thoroughly enjoyed the bath and the swim.

In the morning, we met another family from Wiesbaden. They introduced themselves as Herman and Gabriella Hamburg and their three young children; they were traveling the same way that we were. They also had a homestead, which was only three miles south of ours. It was right on the shore of the Black Sea, and they were very anxious to get to Odessa. Herman played violin and spoke three languages, which included Russian.

We camped together the rest of the way as we enjoyed each other's company. Dad and Herman would sit up late by the fire and talk, becoming good friends and making plans for the future.

As we pulled into the little town of Slenov, I jumped off the wagon and walked up to the feed counter of the livery stable to buy some horse feed. As I did so, Fritz came up beside me wagging his tail. Just then, two men walked out of the store, and

Fritz started to bark. He grabbed one of the men by his ankle; I'd never seen him so angry before. He wouldn't let go of the man's foot. I took him by the collar and pulled him off.

The man said angrily, "Better calm him down before I kill him. Dad replied, "I think you tried that a few nights back."

The man reached for his pistol, and Dad, who was nearly twice his size, hit the guy with a smashing blow. The guy crumpled to the ground and didn't move. Dad had knocked him out with one punch and quickly asked the storeowner,

"Is there a sheriff here in town?"

"*Ya* [yes], I'm also the sheriff 'round here."

"Arrest this man. He robbed us three nights back and stole my watch among other things."

Just then, the other man, who was already sitting on his horse, rode out fast. Dad told the sheriff, "That's one of the other guys that robbed us."

The sheriff took the unconscious man's pistol away and rolled him over. Another small pistol fell out of his boot; it was a Saturday night special. About then, the guy regained consciousness, and the sheriff handcuffed him to the hitching rail.

The sheriff remarked, "Hey, your picture is on the post office wall, along with that guy who just rode off."

He borrowed Dad's horse and rifle and took off after the other robber. In less than thirty minutes, the sheriff returned with the second guy in custody.

"Thanks for the loan of your horse, *mein-heir* [mister]. He's pretty fast. Is this your watch, mister?"

He gave Dad back his watch. Then he took both robbers behind the store to a small jail and incarcerated them. He told Dad to wait because there was a two-hundred-dollar reward for each of them.

Dad told him, "I can't wait. We need to get back on the road." "Okay, I'll pay you now as I can get my money back later." He paid Dad four hundred dollars and shook his hand.

"Thanks a lot, mister. These guys have been causing lots of trouble on the road as you know."

Dad reached over to pet Fritz and said,

"Thanks for the money, sheriff, and thanks for your help too, Fritz.

You've got a good nose."

Dad told the sheriff that there were two more robbers with these men. We kept our eyes open for the others and continued on our way to Odessa.

We would stop when we needed supplies, and Herman would bargain with the shop owners in Russian, often getting us a cheaper price. Sometimes at night, Herman would play the violin, and Dad would join in with his accordion while we all danced to old German songs. Other travelers would stop by to enjoy the fine entertainment and just visit for a while.

I could see that Mom was getting tired of the constant everyday grind, and so I tried helping her with the cooking and washing the dishes. She was keeping a diary of our trip to Russia and always took time every night to make her entries.

Mom was a schoolteacher when she met Dad and continued teaching after my brothers and I were born. She was a big influence on my brothers and me, always making sure that we got a proper education.

We met other families traveling to Odessa in order to take up homesteads around the Black Sea. The migrating families all had the same goals in mind, and we soon became friends with many of them.

The days were long and tiring, and we were all getting anxious to reach our destination. We were forced to trade horses for fresh ones on occasion as our horses were exhausted from the long, hard trip. We usually had to pay ten-dollars exchange for each replacement horse. However, Blackie was ready to go every morning after one night's rest; he always had plenty of stamina.

Everything was going fine until we broke an axle on the wagon. When we stopped to repair it, Fritz began barking loudly. He seemed to be afraid of something up on the hillside. Dad and Xavier were almost finished repairing the axle when I heard a loud yelp from Fritz, and he stopped barking.

Xavier and I took a rifle and scurried off to find him. He was lying in a huge pool of blood with bear tracks all around him. The bear was gone, but we had lost our wonderful pet who we all dearly loved.

The repairs took nearly half a day, so we had fallen behind the other wagons. Just before dark, we came upon a nice campground where many of our traveling companions had stopped for the night; everyone was filled with much anticipation as Odessa was less than twenty miles away.

ARRIVAL IN ODESSA

We arrived in Odessa, our final destination, at 11:30 a.m. We stopped in town for a few supplies prior to going out to the homestead.

Dad kept saying, "How do you like it?"

He was so excited he could not stop talking. "It's beautiful, don't you think?"

Our plans worked out quite well. The entire trip took twenty days, and we were all anxious to explore our new place. As we drew near, Dad candidly pointed out how tall the neighbor's corn was, and we marveled at the other crops that we could see.

As we pulled up in front of our new homestead, we could see a large two-story barn. Mom asked, "Does it have a house, Simon?"

"No, but we'll build a nice, new one for you, right away. Do you think we can live in the barn for a few months while the new house is under construction?

"Yes, but it needs a good cleaning first as it's very dusty and dirty, but yes, it will be fine."

Just then Xavier hollered, "Dad, there's a well and a pump over here, and the water is good. The horses are already drinking it."

"*Vunderbar* [wonderful], Xavier."

We cleaned the barn in less than three hours, and we all thought it would be good enough for a temporary home. Maybe it was not a palace, but after many days on the road and sleeping on the ground, it seemed like a palace to us. At least we could unpack the wagon and have access to our beds and clothing again.

We found an old bathtub and built a toilet, which was soon ready for use. The old cookstove in the barn was heating water quickly, so we all took advantage of nice warm baths. We made do with what we had, and we didn't mind at all.

I picked up some wooden crates from the local market and sat up a temporary kitchen for Mom. She was always content and never complained.

We were finally comfortable in the barn and ready to start building the new house. I couldn't help remembering our nice home on the outskirts of Wiesbaden because it was the showplace of the county. We had lived there for over sixteen years, and Michael was born there. Dad had built that house on eighty acres of fertile farmland, and it was very comfortable.

At first, it was just a two-bedroom house with farmland behind, but we expanded as money permitted and as the family grew. Mom was very artistic and had helped Dad design the entire house. It sat upon a hill overlooking an exclusive section of town.

Things were different now, and we had to start all over by building our new home here on the Black Sea.

CHAPTER II
LAMBERT
BACK TO REALITY

In my dreams, I had escaped reality for the night, but when I awoke at the first light of day, I was back on the battlefield. I could see my Cossack comrades putting on their armor and making ready for battle.

Yesterday seemed only a bad dream to me, but it was real, all too real. In less than an hour, I would be back in battle, fighting for my life again and just trying to survive "The Living Hell" that awaited me.

The Cossacks were all mounted warriors, and since my brothers and I were experienced riders, we felt at home on horseback. We wore protective armor and were always strapped to our horses to avoid being dislodged during the heat of battle. Our sabers were also lashed to our wrists to prevent losing them in battle.

We fought several charges of enemy daily, sometimes without food or water. Our foot soldiers would bring us water whenever possible. They knew that we were their protectors, and they wanted to please us and keep us happy.

Sometimes I could feel my legs being pierced and slashed as we met the charge. There were always loud cries and the pings of arrows bouncing off our armor as the enemy continued to advance. We would retaliate on every charge, usually forcing the enemy to retreat. Once we had them on the run, we would regroup and prepare for the next attack.

My brothers and I often fought together, although it didn't always work out that way. I felt more secure when we were together as we could look out for one another and cover each other's back.

AUTHOR

Many of the Cossacks were notorious fighters from various parts of Eastern Europe and Northern Asia as they had been for many centuries. Their countries of origin were indicated by territorial names attached to their Cossack titles.

They were fearless warriors, and their reputation preceded them. Being such dynamic warriors, they instilled great fear in the hearts of their enemies whenever they engaged with them in battle. They often needed no weapons beyond their famous nagaika whips, which were made of plaited hide. With these whips, they could inflict savage wounds and put the enemy on the run. Quite often, just a few Cossacks could dispel hundreds of protesters.

After they killed or captured the enemy, they often seized the uniforms and weapons for themselves. The Cossacks were most often identified by the way they tucked their pants into their leather boots. There were also female mounted nurses that wore the familiar Cossack fur hats while attending to the medical needs of their warriors.

Typical Eastern Slav Cossacks were noticeably swarthy in appearance with large mustaches while their mounts were shaggy with free-flowing manes. They were very musical and often played a variety of balalaikas and concertinas, usually singing as they traveled along on horseback. They loved to party, to drink wine and vodka, and to dance the gopak, a traditional Ukrainian dance. They would often party for days at a time, displaying their endless energy.

While often deployed by the czar as storm troopers, these fearless Cossacks frequently attacked the enemy on daredevil as well as suicide missions. They often raided, plundered, and confiscating most all their needs. They welcomed fights and brawls wherever they went, and they nearly always prevailed.

HISTORY OF NICHOLAS II

Alexander II ruled as Czar of Russia through some difficult years, starting with his coronation in 1855. He wanted to preserve the foundation of family and state, and he'd been planning to deliver Russia's first constitution. This would have secured them recognition as a civilized European state. Unfortunately, after several unsuccessful attempts, the People's Will assassinated him before the constitution was ratified.

On March 1, 1881, as Czar Alexander II lay dying from an assassin's bomb, he made his grandson, Nicholas II, promise to always maintain absolute power and never abdicate the throne. This memory of his grandfather and the promise he had made would haunt Nicholas throughout his remaining life.

At the early age of fourteen, Nicholas II realized that someday he would be crowned Czar of All Russia. He also knew that he belonged to history, and so he started a diary of his life. He expressed dreams of peace and reform while preparing for the future, but he was ever mindful of the promise he had made to his dying grandfather, to always maintain absolute power and never abdicate the throne.

Alexander III was crowned Czar of Russia in 1881. His family remained intensely fearful of the People's Will. The grounds of the palace were fenced, and guards were placed over the entire compound. The family only left during special occasions and then only while under heavy guard.

Nicholas II, brought up under these conditions, became very shy and timid, which often happens with children of domineering parents. He was very independent and at times considered stubborn, which were remarkable attributes that would benefit him later in life.

This kind and timid boy was unlike the Czar he later became. He received very little affection at home; instead, he was enrolled in the army when he was very young. He was bashful and rarely spoke to anyone. The army meant obedience and discipline to young Nicholas II, which he obviously needed. He began his political career in 1889 with the Council of States and the Committee of Ministers, which was good training for the days that were yet to come.

Nicholas II married Alexandria of the German royal family. Intermarriage with their neighboring countries was common practice in those days in order to ensure political harmony. Marriage to royalty from other European dynasties also secured powerful allies. In the late nineteenth century, the leaders of the three superpowers in Europe were King George V of Britain, Czar Nicholas II of Russia, and Kaiser Wilhelm II of Germany. Being all first cousins, they wanted to keep this power in the family. They felt that their blood ties were a guarantee for long-term peace in Europe, thus avoiding a global war.

Alexandria enlisted the services of a priest by the name of Rasputin, who sought both monetary and political gain for his services. He was thought to have had a spell over Alexandria who in turn influenced her husband and the politics of Russia. This was cause for considerable unrest with the people and was no doubt a contributing factor in the eventual overthrow of Czar Nicholas II.

Czar Nicholas had inherited the throne from his father, Alexander III, when he was just twenty-six years old. Nicholas II was hardly mature enough to command any part of, let alone, all of Russia, and was miserably unpopular.

His absolute rule was not received well by the People's Will as it was too unyielding. They demanded an end to totalitarian rule, and they had wanted it two monarchs earlier. They had enough of this domineering power and wanted nothing less than Parliamentary Rule. Czar Nicholas II sought peace for all throughout Europe and Northern Asia. He was sincere about trying to avoid a global war, which was seemingly inevitable. Despite his efforts of diplomacy, the global crisis would surface in 1909 while Nicholas II was still in power. This crisis encompassed many of the major countries of the world, giving rise to, World War I.

In previous wars, the Cossacks were the heroes of Russia. With the French army in full retreat from Waterloo, Russia, Napoleon was reported to have said, "These Cossacks are a Hoard of Horsemen from Hell." They had brought him to his knees and sent him home in full retreat.

Now, while under Nicholas II, as the strikes and demonstrations raged out of control and spread across Russia, the Cossacks were constantly embattled with the People's Will and were shutting down uprisings as they occurred. Through imprisonment and exiles, the People's Will was disbanded, but the Cossacks became symbols of Czarist oppression.

In the conflicts leading up to and during World War I, the Cossacks continued to support the Russian cavalry and infantry while still fighting alone on many other fronts. They were widely respected by all those that had the misfortune to engage them in battle. Their extreme valor earned the Cossacks the right to be declared, at that time, the most feared fighters in history.

The Russo-German War was helpful in uniting Russia as the entire nation pulled together to back the war efforts of the czar against the German and Austrian armies. Even so, before the end of World War I, freed political prisoners and returning exiles initiated the Bolshevik Revolution.

Czar Nicholas II was soon overthrown and forced to abdicate the throne, giving way to the birth of Communist rule. The close relationship between Czar Nicholas II and his cousins, George and Wilhelm, soon eroded when they made no effort to help Nicholas II and his family during the abdication period. If they had maintained this close relationship and protected Nicholas, it most certainly would have influenced the future politics of Europe.

Soon, Czar Nicholas II was arrested along with his family and his servants. They were isolated from the outside world in the Alexander Palace, where they were permitted to move about only within its confines. Eventually the family was transferred to Ekaterinburg, Siberia.

There they were unmercifully murdered by the Bolsheviks who feared the return of someone from the royal bloodline or someone who could possibly become a martyr.

ANASTASIA'S DESTINY

Some believe that Anastasia, the Czar's daughter, survived the execution, but the story was never substantiated. Those involved told many conflicting stories of the execution, which led many to believe that Anastasia did survive.

Although it is not necessarily my belief, my grandfather believed that Anastasia did survive the assassination that killed the rest of her family. Even though it has remained undetermined for the past ninety years, to my knowledge, this issue is still arguably unresolved.

According to my grandfather, Commander Yurovsky of the execution party decided to remove Anastasia from her family just prior to the executions, telling everyone that she had escaped during the night. This escape was so embarrassing to the execution team who had been charged with guarding the family, that they feared reprisal from their superiors. They simply covered up her escape to protect themselves.

The commander then hid her in his personal quarters to avoid her inevitable death. He was very much attracted to this lovely young Grand Duchess and wanted her for himself. She, of course, was not interested in this old man until he revealed that she would be killed if she didn't give in to his demands.

She soon became pregnant with his child, and the commander decided to move her to a safer place to protect his unborn child. The commander decided to move her to an obscure castle in Germany that was owned by her uncle, Kaiser Wilhelm. After many years of seclusion, Anastasia married Herman Wilhelm, a nephew of Kaiser. She died undiscovered some thirty years later. The child, a boy, was given the German Royalty name of Wilhelm, and his true identity was never questioned or revealed.

I know that this story conflicts with other accounts concerning Anastasia's death, and it may be just as inaccurate as the rest. Still, I have read most of the accounts and have seen Ms. Bergman portray Anastasia on the silver screen. I have also read and heard many experts air their opinions on this matter, but I doubt a verified truth will ever be known.

I would, however, advise that whichever way the pendulum swings for you, to always keep an open mind in your final assessment of this matter. Lambert did!

CHAPTER III
LAMBERT
DAD BUILDS A NEW HOUSE

The first few days were spent getting acquainted with our new place. Dad and Mom were designing the new house while my brothers and I were repairing the farm equipment that had been left by the previous owner. Dad soon started hauling material from town, and we all started work on the new house. I could see the morale building each day as our progress continued. We were nearly finished, and Mom was very excited. It had been an effort of equal enthusiasm for everyone in the family. Just as we finished the roof, it started to rain, but we were ready.

This was a glorious day for all of us as we had just existed in the barn and were not really living there. We all had a dream in our hearts just knowing that we would soon be settled in a beautiful new home again. Dad and Mom were especially thrilled after all the hardship they had endured. Mom was running through the house like a girl with a new dolly, just singing and dancing.

The house was finished in less than three months, and we settled in promptly. It was time to celebrate, so we all sang and danced while Dad played his accordion, and Mom and I prepared a feast.

We planted winter wheat and built some new fences to keep in the horses and cattle. We also planted some fruit trees to enlarge the existing orchard, and then we planted a variety of other trees and shrubs around the house. Soon we had a very attractive and productive place.

The Hamburg family, who we met while traveling to Russia, stopped in to visit us right after we finished building the house. Herman brought his violin, and Dad quickly joined in with his accordion. As before, they played many old German songs. Mom fixed some special snacks, and Dad poured the wine.

The Hamburgs invited us to their place for the following Saturday to have a picnic on the beach as their property was along the water's edge. They had a boat for fun and fishing and spent a lot of time swimming; I was envious.

We left early in the morning for their house, which was nearby and very large. It was not as new as ours, but it was close to the beautiful shore, with large trees and sandy beaches. We boys spent a lot of time walking along the beach, just enjoying ourselves. Dad and Herman went out fishing in the boat, and they soon returned with ten nice halibut. We ate the food that Mom had brought, and Herman cooked the halibut. We all had such a great time.

Herman invited us to come back anytime we wanted, and his wife, Gobby, loved their new home on the beach.

She said, "Please come back again."

We quickly agreed as my brothers and I loved the beach and the swimming. I replied, "We will definitely be back soon."

We were a happy, loving family again like we had been in Germany, with a home, a farm, and new friends. We finally felt that we had arrived. Everyone enjoyed our new home; even

Dad was happy there. We set up a shop to make and repair farm equipment and conduct other blacksmith- type work. Dad, who was very good at this work, was teaching us boys the trade so we could make money.

We spent more time with the Hamburg's and enjoyed their friendship a lot. Xavier went fishing often with Peter, the Hamburg's sixteen-year- old son, and they became very close friends.

One day while they were fishing in the boat, a storm came up and blew them into the rough water. After the storm subsided, they discovered that they were a long way from home.

When the boys didn't come back before dark, Dad and Herman became worried and set out to find them. The boys, who hit land a few miles away, were walking home when they met their fathers. The next day, the boys took the horses and a wagon to bring the boat back home; they didn't go fishing again for a while.

Dad and Herman opened a fruit and vegetable market in Odessa to sell fresh produce from their farms. Sometimes Mom and Gobby would help. Mom made cookies and pies, which were delicious, and they sold fast. My brothers and I sold apples and pears, and we split the money we made. Life was good, and everyone was happy.

We prospered for a few years and began to learn the Russian ways. It still wasn't easy to make Russian friends because of the language barrier. Michael did meet a girl at church with whom he became friends. Her mother was German, so she learned to speak German as a child.

One day, while we were in town, someone told Dad about the political uprisings in Russia. The People's Will, known as the Majority or the Opposition, was seeking parliamentary rule and making demands on the Czar for changes, but the demands fell on deaf ears. The Czar had no intention of meeting these demands. He continued his absolute rule, yielding nothing to the Opposition, and so the situation worsened.

Dad felt much alarm, as we were German farmers, not Russian citizens.

Since we lived on Russian soil, our existence was somewhat in jeopardy.

One evening just before sunset, as Dad, my brothers, and I were about to finish our chores, I happened to notice some men approaching on horseback.

I yelled out, "Dad, someone is coming!"

Dad immediately froze in his tracks when he saw them, as he knew who they were and what they wanted. There were two groups. The larger group stopped, but the smaller group continued to come our way. They carried military flags, so I thought them to be from the government. One man spoke in a loud, Russian voice that I did not understand, but my father did.

Dad answered in an angry voice that shook the ground and then he told us, "Boys, don't move; we have a problem."

Dad told them that we were not Russians, only German farmers, but they didn't care. Again, Dad told them that we were not citizens of Russia. He told them that we were only here on visas and were thus uninvolved in the politics of Russia.

A different man spoke to my dad and raised his rifle as if to shoot. They were making us an offer we couldn't refuse. They ordered Dad to surrender his sons, or they would execute us here and now. This was an offer my father did not refuse.

THE CZAR'S CHOSEN FEW

These kidnappers, who held us at gunpoint, allowed us to take some clothing and say goodbye, nothing more.

A man who spoke German explained that the Czar wanted big men for "his chosen few." They needed to be six-foot-four-inches or taller for the new Russian Cossacks. My brothers and I were at least six-foot-six- inches in height and still growing.

We were quickly tied together with several other tall recruits and were herded off like sheep to slaughter, to fight for the Czar. He was a leader we did not like or respect, and we cared nothing at all for his cause. We had barely escaped the revolution in Germany and had given up so much in order to move to Russia.

There were no warnings that Russia too was unstable and would soon be uprising against the Czar. Most of Russia knew of this problem, but we had no way of getting such information. We weren't able to speak or read the language and had little or no contact with the Russian people in general.

As we continued toward Saint Petersburg, I grew angry, and I spoke to my brothers about escaping at night. Xavier, who was older and much wiser, told me I would most likely be shot.

We soon started Cossack training, a grueling six-week period of discipline and pain. We were exhausted every night, but we managed to continue on.

My brother Michael, being the youngest, was always a source of worry to Xavier and me. He had just turned eighteen and depended on us when he had problem.

I recalled the days when Xavier and I were very young. We would go to town on Saturday nights looking for girls. Sometimes other guys would get mad at us and start a fight. This was a foolish thing to do. We were always so much bigger than they were, and Xavier was a professional boxer. We always prevailed.

Our introduction to the Cossacks was a combination of battle training and conditioning, but above all, we were taught the code of brotherhood. If we displayed anger or disagreement toward another comrade, we would be required to fight that person. These men were all of similar size to my brothers and me and were very worthy opponents. On our fourth day of training, Xavier was afforded the right to fight a rugged, scar-faced comrade named Ivan Vasalov who had stolen his coat and would not return it. The fight was to last until one of the competitors could not continue.

Ivan was taller and much stronger than Xavier, with a fifty-pound advantage over my brother. On the other hand, Xavier was a trained boxing champion who had never been beaten. He was very quick and in perfect condition. Xavier was strong, and he refused to allow this thief to triumph over him. That would only prove one thing, that there was justice for thieves, and Xavier could never allow that.

Xavier avoided Ivan's powerful but less effective punches. Ivan continued throwing powerful blows, but my brother would somehow slip them without any serious effect. Ivan was tiring and seemed to be out of breath most of the time.

The fight seemed endless as they continued slugging it out. The battle raged for nearly an hour, and Xavier was holding his own quite well. Ivan charged in, hoping to get in a lucky punch, but Xavier sidestepped him, avoiding all contact. Xavier came back with heavy blows to the side of Ivan's head. Ivan went down on one knee and shook his head. Xavier went in for the kill, using his feet to deliver several blows to Ivan's ribs. Xavier continued to unload more nasty punches to Ivan's head and neck; it seemed as though Ivan was done.

Then Xavier made a bad mistake; he got too close, and Ivan grabbed his legs. Xavier went down, and Ivan suddenly came to life. They wrestled for some time until Xavier was able to land a solid blow to Ivan's nose. Blood gushed out, and Ivan let go for a second. That was all Xavier needed; he quickly jumped to his feet and landed a dozen or more damaging blows to Ivan's head. Ivan staggered to his feet and lunged at Xavier. Again, Xavier sidestepped, and Ivan missed. He hit the ground with such force that he knocked the wind out of himself.

Xavier moved in once more, and since there were no rules, anything was legal. He landed some final kicks to Ivan's groin, yielding him incapable of continuing.

The coat was returned promptly, and Xavier delighted in his victory.

From that point on, no one bothered my brothers or me.

We continued Cossack training for some time and were taught the hand-to-hand combat techniques for which the Cossacks were so famous. This training indeed saved my life many times in years to come. Once our training was over, we were selected to go to Turkey to fight against the Ottoman Empire where we faced tough opposition. Russia continued to push forward, capturing many small countries in this region. They were expanding their southern territorial borders into the Parmars, a part of the Himalayan Mountain Range that bordered China and India.

We were briefed about our enemy and what to expect in battle. We were warned of their expertise in combat and advised to stay in groups and never to separate from the rest of the troops as they would single out strays and go for the kill. These men were mountain fighters with many caves in which to live and hide. They would fearlessly ambush and attack their enemy, and by no means were they to be underestimated. They were skillful, sly, and tactful. They rode fast horses likened to those of the Cossacks.

The next morning, we engaged in our first battle where my brothers and I rode into the attack. The enemy foot soldiers who foolishly challenged us died quickly. In less than thirty minutes, all of the remaining Ottoman troops retreated into the mountains and virtually disappeared.

Their strong and swift horses did give us some trouble, but we quickly learned how to counter their horse offensive. We held back several of our best horses until all of their horses were defeated or engaged in battle, and then we moved in from the flank, doubling up on them and killing off most of those that were left.

While the enemy was regrouping between battles, Joseph, a comrade foot soldier who always wanted to be a Cossack horseman, often brought me food and water. He fought fearlessly beside me during battle, and his sword was like magic. He had been a foot soldier since his first day of battle. Joseph was the most expert swordsman I had ever seen. He had been trained by a champion in the Czar's Elite Guard, attesting to his longevity in battle.

On one occasion when my horse went down, Joseph was there to cover me against six enemy soldiers until I could cut myself free from my bindings.

As I jumped to my feet, he said, "Welcome, Lambert. You can have these two, and I'll take the rest." As well he did! He soon came back to help me with my two, which he made short work of.

I noticed that Joseph had a German accent, so I spoke to him in German one day.

"Where did you learn to speak German so well?"

He said, "I learned back home in Wiesbaden, where I was born."

It turned out that we were practically neighbors in Germany, and his sister, Adelia, was in my class in school. However, I didn't know Joseph because he was older than me.

The next morning I received a new horse, and he was there to help strap me on. As the day went by, Joseph saw that Xavier was in trouble. He said, "I'll be back soon. I need to go help your brother.

"Okay, I'll see you soon," but I never did.

Xavier told me later that Joseph had fought brilliantly and that he and my brother had driven off many of the enemy. Just as they had the enemy retreating, Joseph was struck in the neck with a hand-hurled spear. He fell at once to the ground, and Joseph—my best friend, outside of my brothers— was dead.

My comrade was killed that day, and I wept. I searched for a reason behind this war, which I could not find. This senseless killing and destruction of humanity was so unbearable that I got sick to my stomach. After dinner, I brought Joseph's body to the camp. Everyone was so sad. I spoke some special words from the heart, and I wept once more along with many of my comrades who loved and respected him as well.

I was devastated!

The conflict continued at a rapid and maddening pace. Only about 10 percent of the Russian Cossacks were expected to survive these brutal attacks, but I was determined to beat the odds.

*****

In the evenings, we would all sit around the fire and tell stories of that day's events in battle. One story that remains vivid in my mind was when a comrade named Boris told of such a frightening experience that I had difficulty sleeping for a few nights.

While we were under heavy attack, Boris was knocked unconscious by an enemy soldier. When he awoke, he discovered that he had been thrown on a pile of dead soldiers.

He said, "I dare not move for fear they would find me out and kill me. I had to lie still for about two hours, waiting for them to leave. I lay there among my dead and bloody comrades until I was finally able to escape."

In another story, soon after we captured a small town, there was a comrade named Aroki who entered the town first. He quickly realized that there were no enemy soldiers left in town. While looking for food and drink, he spotted a small market with no one inside.

He helped himself to some cheese and bread, and then he found a door which lead to a cellar filled with wine and champagne. He quickly grabbed several bottles of wine and returned to the cheese and bread upstairs. After consuming many bottles of wine and much bread and cheese, he passed out for the night.

When Aroki awoke, he found he couldn't move. The market owners were not gone; they were only hiding in the cellar. Once they heard no more footsteps above, they came out of hiding only to find Aroki passed out from too much wine. Quickly they took away his weapons and tied him securely. The shop owners were Jewish and did not believe in killing him; so they dragged him into the street, went back inside, and barred the doors.

These endless tales seemed to help me deal with the fighting and killing.

They somehow kept me in touch with reality. This reality was terrifying and horrific most of the time, which I found difficult to deal with.

On another occasion, a Cossack called Mezeppa told a most unusual story of being under attack by several enemy soldiers. He did his very best to fight them off, but he was soon captured. He was taken to the enemy camp where he was tortured and beaten for hours, but he told them nothing.

He insisted, "I am only a cook, and I'm not trained to fight in battle." At dawn, he was told to help the cook, so he thought he'd do his best. There was a horse that had recently been killed in battle; so he cut it up, boiled it for hours, and served it up as a stew for dinner. The men loved it and kept coming back for more until after dark.

"When they were busy gorging themselves, I quietly slipped away in the dark," he said. "No one came after me, so I kept going all night, and I reached my camp by early morning."

Another comrade told of losing his way after being separated in battle.

I ended up in a small town where the only thing open was a tavern. There was a party with music, dancing, and lots of food and drinks, so I invited myself to the party. No one noticed that I was a Cossack because the locals were all drunk.

The girl serving drinks was very friendly and asked me where I was going.

I told her, "I don't know. I'm lost.

"You can come home with me if you'd like." "Okay," I said, and off we went to her house."

We spent several cozy hours until there was a knock on the door. It was her husband, who had been gone to war for two years, and he was just now returning home.

She told him that I was her hired man for work around the farm. He saw the Cossack clothes and sword but was much more interested in the jug of vodka his wife and I had been sharing, so we all drank ourselves to sleep.

Wisely, I snuck out at the first light of dawn before they awoke, and I was able to get my bearings enough to return to my camp. Most assuredly, I never went back to that tavern again as I might have gotten myself killed.

*****

Finally the enemy stopped charging us. They were hiding in the mountains, so we simply had to follow them. This put us at a sizeable disadvantage as they were trained for mountain warfare. We chased them over half the country but came up on the short end. They could live there indefinitely, evading our movements and disappearing into thin air, making it impossible for us to defeat them.

The czar's troops decided to hold their ground, and eventually there was a standoff. After several months, we were able to convince them to declare a truce. This Russo-Ottoman War was finally over so it seemed. We all returned to Saint Petersburg where the Opposition forces were uprising against the czar. We engaged in fighting around the Winter Palace where demonstrators were firing rifles and canons, to support their troops.

Since my brothers and I were all experienced riders, we were ordered to be part of the cavalry unit assigned to shut down any and all uprisings. This turned out to be an enormous task as we had to cover all of the larger cities in Russia.

XAVIER, MISSING IN ACTION

In the small town of Amorsk, Xavier's horse went down with a broken leg, but his comrades couldn't find him. They reported him missing or captured, along with twenty-five or thirty others.

Once again, the battle slowed down. Some days the Opposition made only one charge over the hill. Then one day it was quiet, and they just stopped charging. We welcomed the silence and the rest, but remained cautious. In a few days, we were told that the enemy had retreated, but we were to stand by on alert.

The captain sent a search party to look for the prisoners from Amorsk. The party returned in a few hours with good news. The prisoners had been set free and were living in town, so a wagon was dispatched to bring them back to camp.

I was full of anticipation as the prisoners returned. Cheers rang out from the returning captives while they kissed the ground and raised their arms to the sky in joyous celebration. I caught a glimpse of someone who looked like Xavier but with a patch over his right eye. He was a little weak and needed help walking, but he looked to be all right.

As I ran to him, I yelled out, "Xavier, Xavier Roth!" He called back, "Lambert! I'm over here."

We had a few moments of hugs and tears, but soon we were able to speak. I asked about his injury, and he told me.

"My horse went down with a broken leg, and everyone had moved on. I was seriously injured and was crying out in German, when a girl nearby who spoke German heard my cries. She took me inside her house, hid me, and cared for my wounds. Her name is Anna, and she moved there from Northern Germany with her parents when she was ten years old."

They have both been killed in the fighting, she said, and now she lives there alone.

"She will soon to be twenty-one and wants to return to Germany, but she is afraid to travel with all the fighting everywhere.

"I love her very much, and we spoke of marriage and the future. I made a promise to her that when the fighting was over, I would return."

XAVIER
XAVIER'S STORY

We lived together for three months in the town of Amorsk, but I was unaware that captives were being held there by the Opposition forces.

Anna told me, "All the Opposition soldiers have left town and have released their captives. Why don't you go out and talk to your comrades?"

I stepped outside and asked a Cossack riding by: "What's going on?"

"The enemy has left town, and the captives have been freed. Are you able to ride?"

"No, sir, I think not, as I'm very weak." "I'll get a wagon to pick you up, okay?"

It was difficult to bid farewell to Anna, so I held her close and reassured her that I loved her. I promised her that I would return as soon as possible.

During my recovery at Anna's house in Amorsk, she told me of a friend, Ejon Vogel, who was with the Swiss Underground. He acted as a courier to send letters to help those who were engulfed in the Russian conflicts and were unable to communicate with family and friends. He would even help to get political prisoners freed, and he offered many other humanitarian services.

He used the churches and the missions as points of contact and had been attempting to help Anna return safely to her homeland of Germany. She told me that we could contact each other through him in case we needed his help. I was happy to know this because I was fearful that I might lose track of Anna. I had grown to love her sincerely, and she remained constantly in my thoughts and prayers. She gave me the name of three missions that he was in constant contact with, and I thanked her for such devotion to me.

I was soon reassigned to a Cossack training camp near Saint Petersburg where I taught Cossack equestrian skills, including weapons and their uses. This training job fit me perfectly as I could finally get away from the senseless killings and regain some sense of purpose.

The recruits were a challenge as they were all seventeen to nineteen years old and completely unprepared to meet the demands that were expected of them, after their training. It was difficult to express my feelings about war, and I prayed that it would all be over before these innocent young men would be exposed to "The Living Hell" that my brothers and I had experienced. Yet

I felt that I was the only one who could prepare them for what to expect and just how to deal with it all.

When the recruit training was over, I returned to my Cossack unit. They sent me to Saint Petersburg to guard the government buildings near the Winter Palace rather than sending me back to battle, back to the slaughter I so hated. We would work twelve-hour shifts, five days on and two days off. We switched between night and day shifts on alternate weeks. Our quarters were in the basement of one of the large buildings. Our uniforms were colorful and tailored to fit. We carried shiny new rifles with bayonets. This was a superb assignment.

My service was only to myself and to my comrades. I didn't care about the czar, but I kept that confidential.

Sometimes we were fired upon by the Opposition, but usually our foot soldiers were summoned to shut down the intruders. We were mostly out of harm's way and not involved in any skirmishes. Upon occasion, we would have to respond when intruders entered the buildings. We always called for help and turned it over to the army when they arrived.

However, we did know how to protect ourselves, that was well established.

We were indeed Cossacks, respected and revered throughout the region.

Everything was back to normal, and it was business as usual in the dynasty of the Romanov's, for Czar Nicholas II and his family.

CHAPTER IV
LAMBERT
MEMORIES

I was still in shock from the stress of the intense fighting during those early days. I would often reminisce about Maggi and those memorable days when we first met.

Early in January, I found myself backed into a hole. The fighting had grown very intense. We lost several horsemen, and the enemy seemed to have the upper hand. My brother Michael and I had fought gallantly all day, but we were outnumbered two to one from the start. As darkness approached, we could see the enemy beginning to retreat. I was struck in the side by a hand-hurled spear that pierced my armor, clipped my right kidney, and finally lodged against my spine. I was bleeding profusely, and my legs were paralyzed, rendering me helpless. I was unable to fight back at all.

Michael noticed that I was slumped over on my horse and came to my rescue immediately, protecting me until the foot soldiers could get there. Without this brotherhood, I would never have survived, and Michael was truly my brother in all respects.

I was quickly taken to a makeshift hospital set up for us in an old schoolhouse near the small town of Lovcheski. I was still unable to move my legs, and I didn't know when or if I would ever recover. I needed extensive medical care and time to heal.

LAMBERT MEETS MAGGI

There were many medical personnel attending to our wounded, including one special nurse who was always helping me and attending to my needs. She was extremely pretty with flowing auburn hair and striking blue eyes. Her name was Magdalena, and she told me that she was from Odessa, I laughed.

"No, are you really? I'm originally from Germany, but now I live in Odessa, that is when I'm home. My parents are living there now."

She smiled and asked, "In what part of town do you live?"

"We live on the Black Sea Trail where my family has a nice farm." "I know the area of which you speak. It is beautiful there." "And in what part of Odessa do you live?"

She told me that she lived near her father's markets in the tourist quarters on Sunset Lane.

"Oh," I replied, "I have been at your father's markets many times.

My family sells fresh produce on Saturdays at the square next door."

"Is that your mother with the good pies and cookies?" "Yes, do you like them?"

"They are fabulous! We probably have seen each other many times before, Lambert, don't you think?"

"Not a chance in the world," I said. "I would remember your pretty face, your flowing hair, and your gorgeous blue eyes. Not a chance," I repeated as I continued to examine her out of the corner of my eye.

"You flatter me, Lambert. I can't wait to meet your mom and dad." "Same here, Maggi. Can I call you Maggi?" "Yes, practically everyone does."

"Your parents must be very special. Are they Russian?"

"No-o-o, me love, not at all. Have you ever seen a Russian with hair the color of mine? No, they are Irish, me dear." I summoned my best Irish accent.

"Irish, is it? Well then!"

We both laughed at my attempt to mimic the Irish. "Then that accounts for your beautiful red hair.

She corrected me. "Not red at all. 'Tis auburn, it is.

"Well, whatever it is, it's like a color from the rainbow, with a splash of sunset that gives it that special glow."

"Thank you for being so kind, Lambert. My hair is quite like me mums, only with a bit more curl, I reckon. My dad doesn't have much hair, but he looks good just the way he is. You'll see."

Maggi and I continued to visit every chance we had. We talked about everything imaginable from religion to politics, and we usually ended up laughing. She asked about my family and what they were all like. She seemed to like everything I told her about Mom.

She said, "Maybe she will teach me to bake all those delicious desserts someday."

She spoke only Russian and Celtic, which didn't help me in the least. My mastery of the Russian language was hardly good enough to carry on a limited conversation with her, and I spoke no Celtic at all. So we made a game of it. I would tell her the name of an item in German, and she would repeat it to me in Russian. Then we would reverse our roles, and she would tell me a different name in Russian, and I would repeat it to her in German. It was fun, and we laughed a lot. It helped me deal with my pain and recovery to which I had been subjected.

I fantasized about holding her in my arms and kissing her. More than once, she caught me staring at her voluptuous bosoms, and she would always give me a cute, little smile in return.

One day while she was bathing me, I noticed her being very flirtatious, and I returned the attention. She planted an exciting kiss on my lips that would have buckled my knees had I been able to stand. Fireworks shot through me like a jolt from a storm, and I knew that I wanted more. I reached for her arm and pulled her to me, creating sparks with every kiss.

This sort of close contact resumed daily while she continued to bathe me and attend to my wounds. Then, one day while we were alone and she was helping me turn over, I felt some tingling sensations in my right leg. I tried moving my toes, and they responded a little.

Maggi asked, "Your leg, it moves, yes?"

"Yes, I think so. I have some feeling in my right foot."

She started to massage it, rubbing it vigorously. She continued the treatment for several days, and then the left leg began to function. The excitement soared, and soon came the big day.

"You will walk tomorrow, Lambert, yes?" "Yes, I will try. I will try very hard."

Expectations were high the next morning as I prepared for my first attempt at walking. She placed two chairs by my bed, and the nurses stood me up beside them while I held on tightly. I struggled to balance on my feet, but I fell down.

"We'll try again tomorrow," Magdalena said.

She began to rub my legs again with much vigor.

The next day I gave another try at walking. I stood up again with lots of help, but on the first try, I fell down again. I tried once more and took three steps before falling. I kept trying and finally was able to take five steps. I stopped while standing erect as everyone clapped.

I yelled, "That was better than yesterday!"

I was moved to a different section of recovery, and Magdalena came by twice a day to visit me in the new ward, but it wasn't the same. We spoke of a future together, and thoughtfully she applied for a weekend pass for me so I could visit her at home.

As we entered her house, she asked, "Do you like my cottage, Lambert?" "Yes, oh yes, I do like it. It's so like you, Maggi."

"Are you pleased that I invited you to come home with me?" I only smiled; she knew.

The cottage was small, like a dollhouse, and I had to duck to keep from hitting my head as I went through the doorways. It was decorated with leprechauns and shamrocks, which left no doubt that she was Irish. She had an assortment of tasty food and wine from her dad's markets, which we soon sampled.

"Magdalena, you are an angel, and I've never known an angel before. God sent you here from heaven to watch over me, and I am putty in your hands."

She smiled, and I knew the feeling was mutual. I hoped we could spend more close time together like this.

"You are so special, Maggi, and I do adore you."

"Will you come to see me when the fighting is over, Lambert?" "Yes, you won't be able to keep me away, my sweet."

As she turned her head ever so slightly, her dimples complimented her beautiful smile, and my heart started to pound. At that moment I could tell that she felt very much the same about me, and I knew that I was smitten by the love bug.

We maintained these wonderful weekend retreats to her cottage, and our romance continued to catch fire. We spent time at the park nearby and walked along the creek, affectionately embracing as we strolled. What a lucky guy I was, and I kept reminding myself exactly how lucky I was to have met Maggi and to have this wonderful relationship with her. During this time, we really connected and expressed our love for each other. I agreed to return upon my release from the Cossacks, and we promised to wait for each other no matter how long it might take.

Oh, how I wanted this terrible fighting to end now, and the sooner the better as I had a renewed purpose in life. Just being with Maggi for the weekends made me so aware of what I was missing. I was missing the whole purpose of life, and all the loving and caring for which I so wanted to come back home to you.

Then, when I returned to the recovery center, I was told that I could return to duty in a few days.

As I returned to the battle camp, I found that Michael was in the next camp. I soon acquired a two-hour pass to go there to see him that same evening. He thought I had been killed by the spear and was so happy to see me. We each shed a few tears and rejoiced that we were both still alive and well.

He was happy to learn of me and Maggi and our plans to marry. He had heard that Xavier had returned to fighting after recovering from a wound to the eye.

The next day I returned to the killing fields, "The Living Hell" that I so hated.

CHAPTER V
LAMBERT
WEDDING

Upon occasion, certain volunteer Cossacks would demand to return to their homes for a reunion with their wives and children. This was a problem as they were mostly from adjoining countries, and quite often they were hundreds of miles from home. If they were told no, they would ride out during the night and not return for over a month, if even then. There was not much the czar's command could do as they were mostly volunteers and not citizens of Russia.

I was, however, still diligently fighting against the Opposition. I continued to immerse myself in these daily battles, and I was struggling just to survive. This demanding stress caused my mind to play tricks on me, making me reminisce about other times and places.

I suffered a debilitating injury and quickly was allowed to return home to recuperate.

After I regained my health for the most part, I became worried that the Cossacks might come after me, or was it possible that they had forgotten about me by this time?

I knew that my brothers were still engaged in all-out combat, and I knew that the war wasn't over. The Opposition still challenged the czar's form of government and demanded an end to his totalitarian rule. They had gained momentum with more power and determination and were continuing their endless demonstrations.

As I gathered my thoughts, I suddenly heard Xavier say, "Lambert, Lambert! Are you all right? Are you ready?"

"Yes, Xavier, I'm ready," I replied as I fought to regain my composure. I was no longer a Cossack in battle. I was suddenly about to take a wife, and she was there, waiting for the music to start the processional. This would be the start of the wedding between me, Lambert Roth, and Magdalena O'Roark, my beautiful Irish bride.

She looked exquisite in her flowing gown while she literally beamed with joy and contentment. This was the big day, the day all young ladies dream about. Magdalena and I were very much in love. We had committed ourselves to each other more than a year ago.

CEREMONY

The ceremony was beyond belief, with meaningful vows and a dedication filled with promises of the future. Even I, the fearless Cossack warrior, was teary eyed with a large lump in my throat. Oh, how I dreamed of this day, this special day to devote my life and love to my darling Magdalena! I loved this wondrous woman to whom I owed my very life. She cared for me as my nurse at first, but now she was my first and only true love.

RECEPTION

The reception was fabulous, and I met so many important people from Odessa that I was genuinely impressed. The mayor and his family were there, as well as several Russian dignitaries from the government. A group of bagpipe performers played typical Irish love ballads with three lovely Celtic soprano singers. Nearly five-hundred guests helped us celebrate this momentous occasion. Magdalena's father supplied the very best food and wine from his gourmet markets in Odessa.

Magdalena held on to my arm as if I were about to escape.

"My dear husband, this is the happiest day of my life, and I'm overcome with love for you. Is everything to your satisfaction, my sweet?"

I couldn't speak, but the smile on my face was the only answer she needed. Finally I said, "You must know everyone in Odessa, my dear."

Now Magdalena smiled, and with a slight nod, she indicated that I was correct. We laughed openly. We cut the magnificent cake, and then we toasted each other with a glass of champagne; it was magical.

"Lambert, you are so handsome in your wonderful wedding suit. I'm afraid to leave you for one moment for fear the other girls might steal you away."

"And you, my dear, are a fairy tale princess that's come to life to marry your prince charming, and I am the luckiest man alive, my love." I smiled as I handed her the poem that I had written especially for her:

Magdalena My Love

There's ne'er a rose that Erin grows
Nor a more elegant sight that I've seen,
Compares to you my beautiful bride
My own precious Irish Cailin. (country woman)
You fill each day with sunlight
You're God's gift sent so serene,
My wondrous wife to cherish for life
You are my angel, my own special queen.
Sure 'tis like a morn in Ireland
When the shamrocks are in bloom,
My heart beats just like a tympani,
When you enter 'nto my room
For your love to me is a symphony
Of a song from your heartstrings,
I cherish your splendor, to you I surrender
And to the happiness that true love brings.

All My Love,

Lambert

"Oh, Lambert," Maggi said. "The poem is so beautiful. I just love it!" We mingled for a while with the guests and shared our happiness with them. Mom and Dad were there with much love and support; they were happy for us. The day was warm and sunny, and the scent of flowers seemed to magnify the intensity of this glorious celebration.

We occasionally stole a polite kiss on the cheek as we scurried to find a secluded corner.

Maggi whispered in my ear so no one could hear.

"Dad has arranged for a beautiful carriage to pick us up soon and take us to a wonderful cottage on the beach of the Black Sea."

I gasped for air and very politely faked a cough. She said that her dad wanted everything to be perfect for us, and so far everything was perfect. I closed my eyes and took a deep breath, for I thought that I was dreaming.

As we continued to thank everyone for coming, I could picture in my mind the cottage on the shore of the Black Sea. Many beautiful places were along that shoreline, and the anticipation of it all distracted my concentration.

Suddenly a glorious, white carriage pulled up in front of our reception area. Maggi's dad whispered softly in her ear, and I was once again overwhelmed by the magnitude of the entire wedding and the thoughtfulness of every precise detail.

I looked at Maggi and found her beaming.

The carriage ride was like the fairy tale, about which I had just been joking.

"Your dad, my love, is a true romantic, and I am forever in his debt." "Should we pinch each other to see if this is just a dream?"

Maggi smiled as she reached over to pinch me, followed by her childish laughter and a kiss on the cheek.

The cottage was more beautiful than I had dreamed in my mind. The rear doors opened onto the beach, and the surf was only about ten steps away. The rising moon reflected on the tranquil waters causing a breath- taking, opalescent hue of uninhibited perfection.

Our gifts arrived at the cottage the next morning, and Maggi asked our servants to help us open them and record who had sent each gift. The next few hours were very exciting. We received gifts, all of the highest quality, from many places. The silver, crystal, paintings, fine china, tapestry, and endless works of art far exceeded my expectations and were much to Magdalena's delight.

We spent a week basking in the sun, mostly sailing and swimming and just absorbing married life and each other.

Maggi asked, "Will you start on our new cottage when we get back to your parents' property?"

"Yes, I think I can start very soon. Dad has offered to help us, and I have the money we will need for the lumber and the other materials."

Dad helped, and we began to build our cottage.

Life was good, so peaceful and perfect it seemed. We made plans for the future, and I went to work for Maggi's father at his stores. He was a great man who was happy to see his daughter in a close, loving relationship. We became good friends instantly, having one thing in common, and that was the welfare of Magdalena.

Just when I was most enjoying my new happy lifestyle, I was notified to return immediately to headquarters in Saint Petersburg. I had been afforded the honor of being selected as an elite guard for the czar and his family at the Winter Palace compound. I was told that because of my spotless record and heroic efforts, I had earned this privilege. This was indeed a great honor as it meant that I had been retired from the killing fields that I so hated, "The Living Hell," that I had been forced to endure. I was promoted to lieutenant and was treated like a hero, which included good food and dress uniforms tailored to fit. The elite guard had white stallions standing by as we were still considered trained killers and Cossack warriors, ready to fight at the czar's command.

I could hear guns and canons outside the palace walls where the czar's troops battled with the People's Will, shutting down uprisings as they would occur. This was the sixth year of such fighting for my brothers and me, and I imagined it would go on indefinitely.

The Opposition mounted an increased offensive on the Czar's Winter Palace in Saint Petersburg. The troops were engaged in all-out war, and the czar's forces were slowly losing ground. The czar and his family were in fear of their lives, so a plan was devised to abandon Saint Petersburg. The word on the street was that an overthrow was imminent and that the czar would be forced to abdicate.

That night, there was a terrifying storm that started right after midnight, and everyone took cover. I, along with the other guards, was awakened by loud clashes of thunder and brilliant flashes of lightning. Suddenly, a messenger appeared and brought us different uniforms to wear.

He told us to hurry, "We're escorting the czar and his family to safety." We quickly mounted our horses and prepared to depart. A carriage awaited

Czar Nicholas and his family at the rear of the castle for a quick getaway. As we formed ranks around the carriage to protect the royal family, the intensity of the storm magnified.

The night was dark, with only flashes of lightning allowing us to find the road on which to make our get away. The rain continued to sheet down, and the thunder continued to roar constantly spooking our horses. The streets were deserted as though all the residents had been banished from this huge city.

The checkpoints had been abandoned by the Opposition troops, which led us to assume that we would have a clear escape. However, as we approached the last checkpoint, which was the main traffic control into the city, we saw a faint light burning, and we expected trouble. The Opposition had taken over this strategic point and posted armed guards there.

The Czar, who was disguised in an Opposition General's uniform, was clean shaven and handed some papers to the guards. The papers introduced him as a general of the People's Will on a top-secret mission. I was ready to charge on command, but to my surprise, the gates opened. The Czar returned to the carriage, and we were permitted to pass. Perhaps the gate guards feared getting drenched, or maybe the sight of thirty armed escorts intimidated them. I felt relieved either way.

In a few hours the storm let up, and the sun shone through on the horizon. As we passed through a small village, some peasants greeted us and brought us food and wine, as well as a new team of horses for the carriage. After we finished our meal, we again hit the road and headed to some unknown mysterious hideout.

I was surprised at how efficiently everything took place, but the Czar had many followers and loyal subjects to aid in his escape. We rode throughout the day until nightfall, and then we were given shelter and food from a man named Abdul. The czar and his family were put up in the house while the guards slept in the barn, except when standing watch on two-hour shifts throughout the night.

At dawn, we were off again for an unknown destination. Two more days of travel followed, and more help was there each time we stopped. On the final day we parted at midday, and the Czar continued on to his secret destination. The guards headed back to Saint Petersburg, guaranteeing maximum security of the czar's hideaway. This maneuver eliminated any chance of betrayal by the guards, who were all kidnapped prisoners of the czar's and were not exactly loyal volunteers.

As we approach Saint Petersburg, we heard lots of celebration. None of the checkpoints still had guards, and the fighting had ceased completely.

I asked a woman who was walking along the road, "What's going on?

She replied, "The czar is dead! We have overthrown the government forces."

We were still dressed in Opposition uniforms, so we attracted no attention as we rode into the city, but I was in shock and feared for my life and the lives of my twenty-nine comrades.

I was on the lead horse on our way back to the palace. I suddenly stopped and raised my arms.

"Attention please, my comrades. We are in grave danger. The government troops have all withdrawn and are awaiting further orders from the czar. We have no more comrades, in Saint Petersburg, to join us."

We all agreed to split up and travel separately to avoid any problems as we were only a handful of Cossacks against twenty-thousand troops of the People's Will.

Soon, I was on my way home, a three-day ride to Odessa. I abandoned all signs of a uniform, but I still had my rifle and saber in case of trouble. I stopped to water and feed my horse, and I was told that the czar had abdicated and that the People's Will had taken over the capital. Still I knew better. I knew the czar was just in hiding and would soon return to his palace home.

As I entered the small town of Ornst, I saw Cossacks everywhere. I stopped and talked to a captain and told him who I was. He then told me that the czar's army was regrouping. They were converging from all over Russia to the capitol and were planning to kill or overpower most of the enemy in the Saint Petersburg area. They would retake the capital for the czar and his family's safe return home.

This was the plan all along, to allow the czar's army time to regroup and to crush the Opposition once and for all. We had been seriously outnumbered and would have sustained irreconcilable losses had we chosen to stay. Now, when we return, we will outnumber them by a two to one advantage. The czar will maintain his power and sovereign rule. As the government troops were better trained and better equipped than the Opposition, our return to the capital was expected to be a bloodbath. The onslaught started before dawn with only a few minor skirmishes.

Our strategy worked superbly, and the Opposition forces scattered and offered little resistance. Surprise was the key to our success, and we regained complete control of the czar's palace. Thousands of Opposition troops surrendered and were imprisoned while the rest were never seen again. I suppose they simply melted into the crowd, offering little or no resistance whatsoever.

We maintained a strong troop count for several days with little sign of the Opposition. Then, once again, the czar and his family were secretly moved back into the palace as if by magic, without being detected.

CHAPTER VI
XAVIER
CEASEFIRE

There were many failed attempts to kill the Czar, but no one got close enough to fire a shot at him or his family. Yet he became a prisoner in his own palace, rarely going outside the compound.

My tour as an elite guard was due to end, and I was offered a chance to stay in the guard or obtain a release. I found the choice easy to make, and I expected to soon be released.

Before I could leave, I was detained once again when the Opposition caused serious difficulties. They made their demands, but the czar did not yield. Parliamentary rule seemed only a dream, and the czar's troops were holding out to the end.

The fighting continued and became much more intense. The losses sustained by both sides were enormous. There was no end in sight; the standoff was unyielding with no sign of victory for either side.

Then at the exact same time, both sides ordered a retreat. Like a preplanned halt to the fighting, with no negotiations or peace talks, both armies ceased to engage in battle; it was like someone flipped a switch.

Day after day, the silence continued while the citizens and businesses returned to their normal daily routine. Everyone suspected that both parties were regrouping for an all-out offensive.

PEACE TALKS

Finally I heard talk of a truce and a mutual settlement. I was told that the czar had offered to negotiate and that he would meet with the Opposition forces, giving in to their lesser demands. In order to avoid more bloodshed, the People's Will was attempting to meet the czar on more common ground, agreeing to decrease their demands. These counteroffers were made to no avail.

Then, as quickly as it stopped, the fighting resumed once again.

We had been on standby for over a month, but now I was alerted to active duty again. The guns roared, and we were once more engaged in a futile effort to obliterate the People's Will, a seemingly endless task. Yet the czar and his commanders offered us no choice.

Many more skirmishes would ensue, and we returned to battle again, back to the futile slaughter of "The Living Hell."

Of course I was away from the front lines, protecting the czar and his family. However, the outcome of every battle was important to me. I desired an end to all this killing and fighting, wishing only to return home once and for all.

CHAPTER VII
MICHAEL
MICHAEL CAPTURED

The fighting started again, and the casualties were mounting. I was seriously wounded, and I did not expect to survive the day. I was surprised by the Opposition, who insisted that I be given the best of medical care, and I wondered why.

After ten days, when I started to feel better, I had a visitor from the Opposition forces' command post. I was advised that they knew me to be German, and they asked me why I was fighting for the czar. I replied that my two brothers and I were kidnapped against our will. They then asked for my help regarding information about the czar's Cossacks, of which I pretended to know very little. After all, I had sworn an oath to the brotherhood of the Cossacks, and I could never betray my brothers or my comrades.

After several days of interrogation, I was able to convince them of my disdain for the czar. I gave them false information that seemed to satisfy them, and I was then placed in a recovery facility with many wounded troops. I spoke very little to them in order to maintain my anonymity and to protect myself as the other wounded soldiers in this hospital were my enemies. It was possible that I had put some of these men in here, and I hated myself for that.

One day I noticed another tall patient who was also wearing a blue armband like mine. He was very quiet, but he eventually spoke to me.

"You are Cossack, aren't you?"

At first I denied it, but I noticed he had a strong German accent when he said, "I know you are my brother."

Again I denied my affiliation. He was relentless and continued to speak to me. Finally one day he spoke to me in German. I tried to ignore him as if I didn't understand him, but I was sure he saw the reaction in my eyes. By now I could tell he was on to me.

I tried to avoid him, but he was always close by.

One day he asked me in German, "Do you want out of here?"

"*Ya,*" I said, "I'm going to escape in three days. Do you want to go with me?"

I was not completely healed from my wounds, but I felt that I could hold my own in an escape.

I pleaded, "Tell me more."

The plan was set; we were to leave through some windows that were left unlocked at night. After 11:00 p.m., the guards were gone, and I felt good about the plan, so we made our exit.

We had been gone for several hours before the guards came back on duty, and by then, we were more than ten miles away. We traveled by night for the first three nights, but we felt safe after that, so we started to travel by day.

We did pretty well by picking fruit and berries to eat. One morning, I was trying to steal some food to eat and was caught by an armed guard of the People's Will. He did not know that I was an escaped prisoner but sentenced me to thirty days of hard labor for stealing.

I was on my way home again but was stopped and questioned by an officer of the Opposition forces. He demanded that I join the People's Will and fight against the czar's government forces.

I told him I was sick, but he showed me no sympathy. I was soon in the uniform of the People's Will, being trained to fight against the Cossacks. The food was good, and I was fed three times a day. What a difference!

I planned to take it easy until I could sneak away and then go home.

I really felt trapped into betraying my brothers and my comrades.

Until now, the Cossack training that I received from my basic training was instrumental in my survival, but the kill-or-be-killed theory was not nearly as effective without the protection of the brotherhood, my Cossack comrades.

Now, everything was reversed on me, and I found myself just trying to survive the onslaught of Cossacks, a seemingly impossible task. I struggled with mortal fear, using all the skills that I had acquired from my Cossack training, determined to stay alive. I avoided contact with the horsemen at all costs, always looking for a chance to escape this bloody reign of hell.

Days, weeks, and months passed; and I was in constant battle. I was frantically trying to survive. Then one day I was shot in the shoulder and rendered helpless. Again, I was back in the People's Will hospital fighting for my life.

MICHAEL MEETS SONJA

Much to my delight, I met Sonja, a wonderful German girl working at the hospital. We talked often, and she told me that she had moved to Saint Petersburg to study at the university. Upon graduation, she was forced to work for the People's Will here at the hospital.

She was not a nurse, but she seemed content working at the hospital. She was good for the morale of the wounded soldiers as she was extraordinarily beautiful and possessed a flamboyant personality. She would bathe me and change my bandages daily. After I began to feel better, we would visit and laugh a lot, and we were quickly becoming friends.

She told me about her beautiful cottage on the lakeshore and asked if I'd like to visit her on Sunday.

I expressed concern.

"Do you think I can get a pass to leave the hospital? I have already consulted my close friend Sarah, and she can arrange it." So I anxiously agreed.

On Sunday she came for me, and I was waiting. She lived alone in the country by the pine forest next to Eliska Lake. It was breathtaking there, and I knew exactly why she loved it. I could hear the frogs and smell the flowers that were blooming everywhere. I was really at peace there.

When it started getting dark, I asked Sonja, "When do we have to return to the hospital?"

"Tomorrow, Michael."

I was surprised but happy to know that I would be spending the night with this lovely creature.

We sat by the fire and exchanged conversation for a while, and then I fell asleep for about thirty minutes. When I awoke, Sonja was lying close beside me, dressed only in a pretty nightgown. I began to talk, and she pulled me to her. She placed one finger over my lips, and I got the feeling that she was not up for any conversation at this time. She kissed me gently, and I eagerly returned the affection. Soon we were locked in an embrace of passionate kissing. We spent the night in splendorous rapture, filled with a feeling of complete euphoria of which I had never known.

We returned to the hospital the next day, and I was anxious for her next visit. We would laugh and sometimes kiss when we were alone. Our love continued to gain ground, and we were both very happy.

On Sundays we continued to spend time together, getting better acquainted, and on Mondays I would go back to the hospital. Soon I was well enough to return to the fighting, to the killing fields, "The Living Hell," that I so hated, but to which I had become accustomed.

Before I returned to battle, I asked Sonja what her plans were after she was released from duty.

"I'd like to go back to Berlin and teach writing and art, at the college level. That is what I've studied to do at the university."

"You know, I would like to spend more time with you, Sonja." I paused for moment.

"Really, Michael?" She smiled and kissed me softly, and I was quick to read her mind.

"Sonja, you know that I love you. Would you like to get married after all of this fighting ends?"

"Michael, do you mean—?"

I interrupted as I was extremely nervous.

"Yes, I'm asking you to marry me when the fighting is over."

She smiled again and softly spoke.

"Michael, I do love you with all my heart. Yes, of course, I will marry you when this crazy conflict is over."

"Wonderful," I said.

She fell into my arms. We relaxed and just talked.

I asked, "Whatever made you decide to move to Russia in the first place?"

SONJA
SONJA'S STORY

In my youth, my mother, my stepfather, and I lived on the Danube River, which flows into the Black Sea and is bordered by many countries including Russia. The Russian language was spoken in the region along with German, Turkish, and a variety of others. This was a good cross culture, where I learned to speak Russian and other languages during my youth.

My mother passed away when I was only eight years of age; subsequently my stepfather, Bernhardt Reichman, raised me from a child and was always there for me. He was a writing professor at the university and was a major influence on me and my passion for the art of writing. After I graduated from the University of the Danube, he recommended that I continue my studies at the university in Saint Petersburg. He had studied there as a young man and knew this school to be outstanding in literature. He also spoke excellent Russian, which he taught me as a child. I found that I would need this desperately in order to study in Russia.

I transferred to Saint Petersburg after graduating from the University of the Danube, in southwest Germany. Upon completion of my master's degree in Saint Petersburg, I was told in no uncertain terms, by the school, that I would not get my degree unless I spent two years of service in the People's Will. I told them that I wished to go home now, but they declined to permit my request. I rebelled against this injustice and told them that I was not a Russian citizen. I demanded to go back to my homeland as my visa had run out.

They told me, "As of now, your visa has been extended for an indefinite period of time."

I had no skills critical to their needs, and I told them so.

"Of what use could I possibly be to revolutionaries?" I quickly challenged. However, the movement had taken over the entire university, and everyone at the school was dedicated to the overthrow of the czar.

At this time I had no options nor did I have any desire to get involved in any Russian political struggles. I had no reason to help overthrow the government of a foreign country. However, I lived on campus, and solidarity was the standard.

I have since determined not to complain since this conscription gave me the opportunity to meet you, Michael. You are a kind, loving, and wonderful man, my very best friend in the world.

I contacted Bernhardt for help, but he had retired from the university and had moved back to Berlin, so he was unable to help me. He is a kind and caring man, and I miss him. He's been a father to me and was so loving and kind to my mother.

He had lived in Berlin as a boy, but Bernhardt had no family left in Germany as they had all immigrated to the United States. He didn't speak good English, so he declined to go to the United States with his sister and her husband. Bernhardt also played cello in the Berlin Symphony Orchestra and did not wish to give that up. He had played for many years in the Danube, where I think he began shortly after my mother died.

Eventually his nephew, Peter Koonz, invited Bernhardt to live with him in Berlin.

MICHAEL

Sonja and I made plans to meet in Berlin, a town where we were both familiar. She gave me the name and address of her stepfather, who agreed to act as liaison, keeping us both informed of each other's whereabouts. I could rarely get or send mail because of my affiliation with the Opposition, but he always had Sonja's latest address.

Our plans were to marry at Saint Christopher's Cathedral, where we were both acquainted and at a date to be determined. This church was only a few blocks from the train station and very easy to find.

This task turned out to be much more difficult than we ever expected. After I returned to battle, I sent a letter to Sonja's stepfather, Bernhardt, and I received one in return. Sonja had been moved to Moscow where she was assigned to the administrative section of a large hospital. I was happy to know this and quickly sent her a letter. My letter was soon returned to me, and I figured that Sonja had been transferred once again. This was all very difficult as we both worked for the People's Will, but the government was the only source for mail service, which made it very hard to contact one another directly within Russia.

In a few months, I received shocking news in a note from Peter Koonz, Bernhardt's nephew: his uncle had died of a heart attack.

I responded immediately, knowing all too well the urgency of establishing this new contact in the role Bernhardt had played. I sent Peter all the information he would need to keep me informed of Sonja's whereabouts.

He did not respond. My spirits sank to a new low, and I did not know where Sonja was or how to contact her. My only hope was that Peter would eventually contact me or my mother, whose address I had also given to him.

Peter never answered any of my letters, and I had a feeling that he was not going to. I tried to think of other options since there was always a chance that I could locate Sonja in other ways. I could go back to the hospital where we met or to her lovely cottage. If all else failed, I could go back to Berlin, to the address of Peter Koonz, to see if I could find him. I could even check at Saint Christopher's Cathedral and show Sonja's photo around.

I certainly was not about to give up. I would search to the ends of the earth to find her.

My love for Sonja was so sincere that I could not possibly continue my life without her. She definitely was God's gift to me, a gift so precious and genuine, and I knew that she had the same feelings for me.

After many months of zealous fighting, the intensity was winding down again, and I figured that I could make a clean break soon.

Where would I go? What would I do to find Sonja? My innermost thoughts were that she seemed to have vanished.

In less than two weeks, I bid farewell to the People's Will and quietly slipped away. I don't think they ever missed me as there was little or no fighting at that time. There were rumors that the czar was yielding to some of the demands of the People's Will, but I wasn't sure just what was what.

With an uneasy feeling of loss, I readied myself to search for Sonja, which could possibly take years. I would never relent on this mission, short of death, I told myself.

I was able to travel more freely now, and I decided to go back to the hospital in Movorka, the small town where Sonja had lived. I had to see her, to reassure her that I was okay and that I still loved her, to inform her that I was no longer a soldier and belonged to no man's army.

As I approached the hospital where I had met Sonja, I could see it was closed, for there was no one around. I went to the market where Sonja and I had shopped before and asked if they knew where Sonja was. They sent me across town to a small hospital where I asked for Sonja. They told me to wait while they went to get her. Soon she appeared, and when she saw me, she nearly fainted.

"Sonja!" I shouted. "At last I've found you!"

"Michael, my dear, Michael, is that really you? I heard that you had been killed."

We embraced, and she cried. I held her close and kissed her. "Michael, please wait. I will be able to leave in just a few minutes. I must sign out."

I agreed and soon found her nestled in my arms at her house by the lake.

"I heard that you had been killed near Saint Petersburg several months ago. I've been so upset and have cried practically every moment."

I told her that I had been in battle and in the hospital since I was with her a year ago. I had found it impossible to send or receive mail.

She continued, "Shortly after I heard that you had been killed I met Petrov, another wounded soldier. Petrov is a wonderful man who was here until one month ago when he was released from the People's Will. He was injured and unable to continue fighting. He asked me to marry him one day, and I thought that since you had been killed, it would be okay. I was terribly lonely and found it difficult to continue on.

Then Petrov received a letter from his old girlfriend in Saint Petersburg, professing her love for him. He told me that he needed more time to decide and that he wanted to go see her. He said that he would return in four weeks to give me his decision. Tomorrow will be the end of the four weeks, and I don't know whether he will return or not.

"Now I am the one who needs to decide, that is Michael, if you still love me."

I hesitated for a few seconds. Naturally I was in shock to think I might lose the girl of my dreams. I was speechless, and I found myself stammering just to find the words to reassure her of my love for her. As I stood there growing pale, I noticed tears in her beautiful eyes, those soft, caring eyes that I so adored.

"Yes, Sonja, I do love you, and I always will."

I could see that the situation was very delicate, and I just wanted to make certain that she knew I loved her. I had never seen this caring and emotional side of Sonja before, and I had forgotten how absolutely gorgeous she was. I suggested that I stay at the inn until Petrov returns. "No, my friend, Helena, has a place for you across from the hospital.

Please don't go until the issue is settled."

I agreed to stay while Petrov made up his mind, which would be very soon. We kissed, and we found it difficult to part, but I agreed to meet her in the morning for breakfast. I was extremely restless all night contemplating this delicate outcome.

I asked myself, *What do I do now? Should I ride out, or should I wait for Sonja to see this through?*

I awoke at the first light of dawn and discovered that the answer to my quandary was no longer an issue. Sonja was already sitting in the kitchen talking to Helena.

As I entered, I casually interrupted. "Good morning."

I could smell the aroma of fine food wafting in the air, causing my juices to flow. I quickly asked, "Did you sleep well, ladies?"

Sonja replied, "No, I didn't sleep at all."

Helena asked, "Would you like some breakfast?"

"Okay, just as soon as I get a good morning hug from my favorite girl." We conversed and nervously enjoyed the delicious food.

I asked Sonja, "Are you okay, my love?" She smiled and reached for my hand.

I took her in my arms again and held her close. I whispered, "I love you."

She smiled and kissed my cheek.

"Michael, I'll come here tonight immediately and tell you what Petrov has decided. I hope that he does not return because, Michael, you are my choice, no matter what he decides. I love you and want to spend my life with you."

I started to choke and could not speak for a few seconds. "Are you sure, Sonja? If you need more time, I'll understand."

As I spoke these words, I knew how she was feeling. I also knew that Sonja had thought me dead and had suffered emotionally, and that bothered me considerably.

Maybe I was the one who needed more time to examine my feelings now. Did I really love her, or was I just caught up in this love triangle that was now unraveling? Did I love her enough to marry her? I only had a few hours to decide, but in my mind the answer was very clear.

I was growing anxious, and all the time I was waiting for Sonja to return from work and break the news. What would she decide if Petrov chose her? I found myself shaking with nervous tremors, and I was pretty sure my heart was skipping a few beats while my head seemed to be floating far above my body.

Just as Sonja was to get off work, Petrov rode into town. This was nearly a cause for a stroke as I was standing there by the side door of the hospital waiting for Sonja when I saw him greet her. She did not hug or kiss him, to my relief.

I went back to Helena's and waited for Sonja; that was all I could do. It seemed like hours, but after only about twenty minutes, Sonja came to me with her news.

"Michael," she most excitedly declared as she trembled noticeably. "Petrov is going home tomorrow, and he will marry his old girlfriend.

I told him that you were very much alive and that I still loved you. This made it easier for both of us even though I could see he was very disappointed. He never said, but somehow I felt that he wanted to stay with me. He insisted that he was happy for me and wished me well. Is this what you want too, Michael?"

My heart was pounding out of control, and tears started to roll down my cheeks. At that moment I knew this was real love, and I definitely wanted Sonja to be my wife, to love and hold forever. I'd never wanted anything so much in my life. I reached out my arms, and we embraced.

"Yes, Sonja, that is what I want too, more than anything else."

She told me about spending three months in Moscow on administrative duty. However, they closed the hospital and sent her back to Movorka. I explained to her about a letter I received from Bernhard, where he informed me of her transfer to Moscow, but the letter I sent to her in Moscow was returned to me unopened.

I told her that I must go now to bid my mom and dad farewell before they depart for America. She was aware that I hadn't been able to contact them for over a year and that they needed to know that I was alive and well. I told her that I would return as soon as possible.

Then I held her close one last time. We kissed and parted.

CHAPTER VIII
XAVIER
XAVIER, ALIAS FATHER JAMES

On my travel to Amorsk, I went to the cathedrals for food and shelter. Then one day a priest told me to be careful because the fighting had started again and it was not safe to travel. He gave me a robe and collar for a disguise. He also gave me a Bible and some papers that identified me as Father James Boyco, which explained that I was traveling to school.

He said, "This will help you travel."

I had gone to seminary school in Germany about six years earlier and had a good knowledge of religion. Since then, the German Revolution, the bloody Russian war games, and now the endless uprisings had left me unable to finish my studies.

I was forced to travel by night toward Anna's house in the town of Amorsk, and I managed to avoid attention for about seven days. I had in mind to reach Anna in about thirteen days, so I pressed on.

We were both using Ejon Vogel of the Swiss Underground to help keep track of each other. Ejon could travel freely with only his Swiss passport, but Anna and I were German citizens and did not have that luxury. Ejon and I met at the mission in

Bakavich, and he gave me a letter from Anna. She had sent some pictures of a little boy named Xavier Junior, my son, now nearly two years old, whom I had never met. I was overwhelmingly happy to know that I had a son, a beautiful child who displayed many family resemblances. I couldn't wait to meet him.

I gave a reply letter to Ejon, and he said that he would deliver it to Anna in about a week. I expressed my thanks and bid him farewell. As I continued to travel, I left my alias where I was staying in order to give Ejon a better chance to follow my progress.

There were soldiers everywhere I turned, but I had them convinced that I was a priest. I continued to travel through the roadblocks and was questioned often. I was afraid of these men because they were Cossacks but no longer my comrades.

One day I was stopped at a roadblock checkpoint while my papers were examined. I was questioned in Russian, and I promptly answered in Russian. They saluted me, as Father James, the priest, in a military manner. They laughed, and I did the same; all was well.

The next checkpoint was similar, and they again checked my papers and questioned me. Everything seemed all right, but a captain sent word from inside the building to send me in to his office.

I noticed that he was very tall, and as he reached for the light over his desk, I was horrified to see a familiar face. This giant was my worthy opponent during Cossack training, the man I beat in a fight over my stolen coat, Ivan Vasalov. He was hardly a friend, and I hoped that he would not recognize me as he might cause me trouble.

XAVIER IMPRISONED BY IVAN

He began to interview me, asking my name and place of birth, and the usual questions. I kept my voice soft and low, trying to maintain my stability as I knew a priest would do.

"Have you ever been in the military service?"

The blood shot through my veins, and I feared that he might have recognized me. I answered him quickly, "I'm a man of God, not a warrior, sir."

Ivan briskly responded, "I'm a soldier. I'm a Cossack."

The words echoed through my brain as we both stared at each other. "Do you think God will forgive me for killing in the war?"

"That's between you and God."

"Why did you not become a Cossack?" Ivan softly asked. "You are very tall."

I made up a story that I was in seminary school, studying to become a priest, which was why I'd not been in the Cossacks. Ivan just stood there looking at me, and all the time I was about to collapse.

I wondered if I was going to have to fight him again. "You will be my guest here and teach me about God, yes?"

I suggested that I go home first to see my dying father and come back in a few days.

"How do I know you'll return in a few days?"

Speaking as, Father James, I calmly replied, "You have God as my witness. What more could you ask?"

Ivan looked confused, and he didn't answer right away. Finally he said, "No, I like it better my way. You will be my guest and teach me now!"

I didn't dare ask Ivan how long I would be detained because he was a very mean and notorious killer. However, I was sure that he did not remember me or the fight we had in Cossack training.

It followed that I had a Bible with me, and I started to teach him about God. Ivan seemed only minutely interested, and I felt like I was talking to a rock. At night I was locked in jail for safekeeping, but I was fed very well and treated kindly. During the day I taught and read the Bible continually to Ivan, explaining as I went along.

After eight months as Ivan's prisoner, word arrived that the fighting had ended. I assumed Ivan would soon be departing, and he would finally release me. The next morning after breakfast, I noticed that he did not send for me.

I asked the guard, "Where is Ivan?"

"He has been called home as his father is in grave condition." "Did he say that I could be released?" "No, he did not say."

I replied angrily, "When will he return?" "He left no message pertaining to you."

Upon that note, I was no longer Ivan's guest. On the contrary, I was his prisoner, left here to rot in his cell until this madman returned. I decided to discontinue teaching him anymore when he returned. After all, I was James the priest, a man of God. I was sure he did not recognize me as Xavier Roth.

I was feeling more dejected by Ivan's failure to release me as time went on, and I started to look for a possible escape. Four weeks had passed since his departure for home.

I asked the guard, "Has Ivan returned yet?" "No, Father James, he has not."

My patience had become completely exhausted while I was confined to this dungeon. Was this my ultimate reward for doing God's work? I pondered. What should I do next? Anna would surely think I had been killed by now, or maybe she's gone off somewhere and gotten married. If I ever get out of here, I vow to search until my dying day for this woman that I love.

As I lie there, wasting away in that prison, I realized that my situation must be part of God's eternal plan. He has a purpose for me, so I must learn to be more patient and to have faith. I told myself that he will deliver me when the time is right and not one day before.

In just a few days, I learned that Ivan was back. I was not too pleased with him, but he held the key to my release, so I must show him respect.

The next morning, the guard opened the gate to take me to Ivan's quarters. I calmly followed him.

When I saw Ivan, I muttered, "Welcome back."

He looked at the floor and replied, "I'm sorry that I was gone so long, but my father was sick, and now he has gone to be with God. Are you angry with me?"

"Ivan, I have been punished by you, yet I have committed no crime.

Please tell me, do you think this is justice?"

Ivan looked as though he was sincerely sorry.

"Please forgive me, James. I'll make it up to you soon. I promise I will." While we spoke, I could feel much sincerity in his voice that I had never known before. He then confided in me that his father had died, and he softly said, "But not before I had introduced him to the Lord our God. Thank you for that and for your teachings of love, peace, and forgiveness, James."

And now I knew why God had allowed me to suffer in anguish in that prison cell. My faith was renewed, and I was finally at peace.

He told me that God had forgiven him and had blessed him with joy in his heart. Then he confided, "I am now a peaceful man, and I can be happy at last, thanks to God and your teachings."

My heart raced, and I was worried now that Ivan didn't need me anymore. I calmly asked, "Ivan, what are your plans for me?"

He smiled, and a feeling of relief came over me. "I know who you are, Xavier. I've known from the start. I only kept you here to protect you and for you to teach me about God. I also knew that God was angry with me, but you see, I can't read or write, and you can. I needed you to teach me about God." "We are both Cossacks," Ivan continued, "and bound by our brotherhood code, which makes us comrades for life."

XAVIER AND IVAN MAKE PEACE

Ivan said, "I will release you now, and to show you my appreciation, my men will escort you safely to Amorsk."

"God will bless you, my comrade," I reassured Ivan.

We exchanged the traditional farewell with a hug and touching of both cheeks in Russian style, and I was choked with emotion. I knew my teachings of God and love had been heard by this hardened warrior, and that indeed was a good feeling. I felt that I had made a true comrade of my one-time adversary who was now a true brother of the soul, and I was filled with jubilation.

Ivan spoke again, "Xavier, if you ever need my help for anything, I can be reached at the border town of Dresden, Germany. You can contact me at 2721 Harbor Strassen, anytime."

We parted and I was a little sad, but I appreciated the fact that Ivan had offered to help me if I ever needed him. Who knows what the future holds?

CHAPTER IX
XAVIER
ANNA'S HOUSE FIRE

Before being detained for ten months, I had sent Anna a message that I was only seven days from her house. Now, I would soon be on my way once again. I was anxious to see my love and spend some quality time with her and our son. At this time, I was only three hours away and was shedding tears. They were good tears, tears of joy.

As we approached Anna's house, I saw some flames and some smoke coming from her roof. My heart sank. The house was ablaze and nearly gone. As I stared at the remnants, I had this empty feeling, and I wondered if they had escaped the fire. Then I looked at the bakery next door where Anna worked, and it was destroyed too.

I was at a loss with nowhere to turn. I told the men who escorted me that I'd take it from here.

They said, "No, we'll help you."

We scoured the town, but we couldn't find anyone who could tell us a thing about the fire. I left feeling distraught.

I went to the mission, and I asked them to contact Ejon, hoping to find out where Anna had gone. He knew nothing about the fire but said that he would investigate and get back to me.

I stayed there for another two days and thoroughly searched the town, but Anna was nowhere to be found. She couldn't know that I was all right and had been released from the Cossacks. She couldn't possibly know that I was searching for her.

I walked the streets every day, asking about her and the boy, but got nowhere. I went back to the burned-out house and left a note on a large wooden box that could easily be seen. I told her that I was in Amorsk looking for them and that I would be staying at the mission.

I knew my family must be worried as I told them ten months earlier that I'd be back in about thirty days. With a heavy heart, I reluctantly headed back to Odessa. This time I could travel more freely as I had my release from the Cossacks. I traveled mostly by train as Xavier Roth, not as James the Priest, and I made remarkably good time.

BON VOYAGE TO MOM AND DAD

I finally arrived at home in Odessa just in time to tell everyone goodbye. I told them I had to go back to Amorsk to find Anna and the boy, and then I'd come to New York just as quickly as I could get everyone together. I spent some time with Michael, who was also home to bid everyone farewell. Sonja could not leave Russia for two more months so that would give Michael time to renew his visa.

Lambert had also gotten his release from the Cossacks and was leaving along with his family to go to New York City with Mom and Dad. He discovered that he didn't have enough money for his passage after buying tickets for his wife and their three boys. He was able to get a job loading cargo on the SS Guggenheim, the same ship on which his wife and children were departing for America.

He planned to work for about four weeks, and then he'd have enough money to join his family in America before his visa ran out.

LAMBERT

I spoke to the cargo foreman and asked him for a job. He asked, "What can you do?"

I told him that I could do more work than any two men that he had. He offered me twenty dollars a day, and I countered his offer, "Make it thirty dollars and pay me every day."

"Okay," he said. "But for twelve hour days." I agreed, and he replied, "Let's get started."

We only had three days before the ship's departure, and they had a big loading crew. I worked hard for two days, and on the third day, he put me in charge of loading huge barrels of pickled herring. Near the end of the day, we only had about twenty more barrels to load. I loaded nineteen barrels full of herring, but the last barrel was empty. I went aboard with one friendly worker to tie them down.

I told him, "I'm going to crawl inside the empty barrel. You put the lid on it, but don't fasten it down."

We only had a few minutes before the ship was to depart, so my coworker walked off the ship alone, and I was all set for a free ride. After we were up to full speed, I jumped out of the barrel and closed the lid to avoid any suspicion. I simply walked out on deck where the passengers were mingling, and no one suspected a thing.

I knew the cabin number of Maggi and the boys, so I knocked on their door. They were really surprised to see me as they didn't know that I planned to stowaway. I got a free ride, which saved me nearly $300, and no one was the wiser.

When we arrived in New York City, I went through customs with Maggi and the boys and showed them my visa. There were no problems; all went well.

Mom was almost eight months pregnant when she and Dad left Russia, and she was really concerned about traveling at that late date. She was quite upset with Dad about his lack of concern for her condition, but he said that they must go before their visas expire. If they have a problem, they might never get out of Russia.

As the ship pulled into London Harbor on November 20, 1899, to offload and pickup new passengers and cargo, Mom started having labor pains. Dad took her immediately to the Mission of St. Peter's Hospital, to deliver the baby. He was able to get an emergency visa extension for her to stay over, but they would not give one to anyone else in the family. The mission provided free care for Mom and the baby until they left again for New York.

In less than twenty-four hours, the rest of us were back aboard ship and headed for New York. Our estimated arrival date was Christmas Day at 4:05 p.m. We planned to stay at Uncle Anthony's house on Long Island while we waited for Mom and the baby to arrive.

So far, the voyage from London to New York was quite enjoyable for everyone. We cruised along at top speed, and soon we were only a few hours from Ellis Island in New York Harbor.

Someone was calling out for Mr. Roth, and Dad supposed that it was news about Mom. He went to the ship's office and told them that he was Mr. Roth. They said that they had found his lost son.

Dad, thinking that it must be one of my boys, told them, "Okay, bring the boy here."

Soon a boy about four years old came out, but Dad didn't know him. He told the mate that this was not his son. Dad had started to go when a lady arrived and told them that she was Mrs. Roth and was looking for her lost son.

Only observing, Dad waited there until the lady started to leave with the boy. Dad spoke to her and told her that he was Mr. Roth.

She laughed and asked, "Do you think that we are related?"

Then they both laughed, and she told Dad that the boy's grandfather was killed in the war, over twenty-five years earlier, and she believed that it would be impossible for him to be his grandfather. They both smiled and said goodbye, and then they quickly parted. They never crossed paths again on the ship.

When Dad returned, I asked him, "What was that all about?"

Dad told me the whole story about the lady and the boy. We thought it was sort of peculiar, but Dad said that there were many Roth's in the world.

We finally arrived on Christmas Day after spending about a month on the *SS Guggenheim*. Christmas in New York was a spectacular sight. We were all amazed by the grand celebration gala with the colorful lights and fascinating music. Central Park was a winter wonderland with a light coat of new snow and decorated trees. People were skating everywhere on the ice, which was really exciting to watch.

Our cousins took us to Times Square where there were nearly ten thousand people and then to Coney Island where everyone had fun on the carnival rides. We all had the times of our lives eating hotdogs, popcorn, and all the many other delights that were so very new to us. The cotton candy was my favorite of all, and the hot dogs were Xavier's favorite.

What a far cry from the life of a Cossack Warrior, I thought. I didn't know life could be so enjoyable. We were in a different world where people were kind and caring, not bent on destroying each other.

At age twenty-five for me and twenty-six for Xavier, we had known more pain and hardship than most people would endure in a lifetime. We had been in battle for nearly six years and had each cheated death several times.

Yes, America was *vunderbar*, more wonderful than I had ever imagined. It was like a dream come true. As we enjoyed New York City and our family, who were our guides and translators as well, I felt such an overwhelming feeling of contentment. I was at peace.

We had traveled thousands of miles to reach the New World, and it truly was a new world. As I pondered in disbelief, I told myself that Dad was right, *America is wonderful.*

When we arrived at Uncle Anthony's house, we received a telegram from the American Red Cross:

To: Simon Roth,
Congratulations,

You are the father of a six-pound four-ounce baby girl. Stop. Mother and baby are doing fine. Stop. The baby's name is Helen Olga Roth. Stop. She was born at 10:21 p.m., November 21, 1899. Stop.

THE AMERICAN RED CROSS

Celebrations were in order. Uncle Anthony had some champagne, and we all enjoyed the music as Dad and his brother sang and played. Everyone was so happy that Mom finally got her girl.

We were expecting Mom to arrive with the baby in New York City between January 13, and January 15. We planned to contact immigration soon to get Mom's exact departure and arrival times.

A snowstorm greeted us on the third day after our arrival, allowing us to spend much time romping about like children. We also spent time fishing off the Long Island Pier where we caught some nice codfish. We bought some clams at the marina, and Aunt Olivia made us some chowder; a great new dish we had never experienced.

We were counting the days until Mom's arrival. It seemed like months, but she did have to wait for the next ocean liner leaving for New York. We checked, and her arrival date was on January 13, 1900. Her ship was The Celtic Liner, with 2,857 passengers. It would arrive at Ellis Island at 2:00 p.m.

We were all so excited to see Mom and our new baby sister. Everyone was at the harbor and eager to welcome our newest family member. It took nearly an hour before Mom appeared, even though she was the first one off the ship and through customs. The ship's nurse carried the baby, and Mom was waving and calling out Dad's name, "Simon, Simon, Simon!"

She was really excited as the nurse handed the baby to Dad. Then we all took turns holding her for a few minutes while Mom hugged everyone.

She asked, "Did I do a good job?"

We all clapped our hands, and we headed for Long Island. Mom, Dad, and the baby all rode with Uncle Anthony in the carriage while the rest of us rode the train to Long Island and walked from there as it wasn't very far. We stayed another two days while Mom and the baby rested for the trip to South Dakota.

We made reservations to take the train to Aberdeen, where we planned to live. Dad wanted to buy some land to build another house right away, close to his brother, Edward.

When we arrived in Aberdeen, Uncle Edward met us. He had a job for me that included a nice house. It was only four miles from Uncle Fredrick's farm. We all stayed at Uncle Fredrick's until Dad found a place of his own nearby.

We were all concerned about Xavier and Anna, who were expected to arrive soon. They had been separated from each other during the fighting and were searching for one another desperately.

South Dakota was a great place where everyone was friendly and helpful to each other. We grew to be very fond of these wonderful prairie people.

XAVIER

While I was on my way to look for Anna, the fighting started again. I was caught at a checkpoint and given a job training new recruits for the Cossacks. I was not happy over this highly illegal maneuver by the Russian government to detain me once again. I had a visa to enter the United States, one that Dad had obtained for each member of the family, and I protested feverishly. Since I was not a Russian citizen and had a legal visa to travel, they were violating my rights, and I continued to protest aggressively.

My visa was good for ninety days. If I could get released from this latest training camp assignment, I still had time to find Anna and the boy and to get their visas in Germany before mine expired.

I continued to demand my release from the Cossacks. I showed the Russian Immigration Service my visa to the United States, which indicated my intentions to leave Russia. After sixty days of training recruits, I was suddenly given my release and told to leave Russia within thirty days, the date when my visa would expire.

I agreed to leave and was soon on my way to find Anna and Xavier Jr. I had been in Saint Petersburg, which was only one day's travel from Amorsk. Excitement filled my entire being, and as I departed, I wore my priest's clothing for protection.

On my way to Amorsk, my mind started to run wild.

Is she still alive? I asked myself aloud. I wondered if she was still living in Amorsk.

I quickly went to the mission to see if I could find Ejon or Anna, and I checked to see if they had left me a message. Ejon had sent a message telling me that he would see me on Friday this week in Amorsk. Today was Tuesday, and Anna had not been there at all, so I was on my own until Friday. I was excited beyond belief, just knowing that at last I would find Anna and my son.

I returned to the burned-out house to find the note where I had left it. I started looking for Anna again, asking in the shops around.

After an exhausting day, I tried a shop near the center of town called the Garden Market. The man I talked to recognize their photo and told me that they always came in on Friday afternoon about four or five in the evening. I found myself consumed with excitement, and I thanked him. It was now Wednesday, with only two days to wait, but it seemed like an eternity.

I was anxious when Friday finally rolled around, so I spent all morning at the market just waiting and watching in case they happened to get there early. It was now two o'clock, and then four. At a quarter to five, just as the sun was starting to fade, I noticed a boy who was bouncing a ball in the street in front of the market, but he looked older than Xavier Jr.

There were several doors going into the market, and I thought perhaps I could have missed Anna when she entered.

As I approached the boy, I softly said, "Hello." He replied in German, "Hallo."

I was about to ask him his name and just then I heard a woman's voice say, "Xavier, where are you?"

"I'm out here, Mother."

As he started to leave, I asked him, "Is your mother's name Anna?" "Yes it is! Do you know my mom?"

I began to tingle with excitement when I saw Anna step from the front door onto the walk. She couldn't see my face, but only that I was talking to her son.

She anxiously asked, "Can I help you?" I turned, held out my hand, and said, "I love you, Anna."

She almost had a heart attack as she thought that I was a priest because of my clothing. When she screamed, little Xavier thought I had come to harm them, so he started hitting me to protect his mother.

I let out a rather loud laugh, and Anna knew instantly who I was. She grabbed my outstretched arms and started to hug and kiss me. Xavier Jr. did not know who I was, but he quickly discovered that I was a friend.

Anna told the boy, "Xavier, this is your father, and he has come to live with us."

The boy looked like my dad: long legs, blonde hair, and blue eyes. I picked him up to hug him, and I kissed him on the cheek. He smiled and gave me a big hug.

He said, "Hallo, Papa."

I told Anna that I had been looking for her for nearly two months.

We finished shopping and went next door for coffee at Dimitrio's where Anna told me her exciting story about the fire and her brush with death:

ANNA
ANNA'S STORY

In the early hours of the morning, I was restless, so I got up to get a drink of water. As I walked through the kitchen, I could see flashes of light coming through the curtains. Upon investigating I could smell smoke, and as I peered through the window I was able to see that the bakery next door was engulfed in flames.

My heart nearly jumped into my throat, and I quickly ran toward Xavier Jr.'s room, which adjoined the bakery. The ceiling was ablaze and starting to crumble.

I yelled out, "Xavier! Xavier!"

As I reached his bed, I saw that it was empty; I called out again. "Xavier, where are you?"

By this time, the room was filled with dense black smoke, and I started coughing profusely. I got down on my knees to look for him. Then I heard him cough over next to the exterior wall.

I called his name once more, "Xavier!" He coughed again.

I could barely see him slumped in the corner as I caught his movements. Just as I reached him, a section of the ceiling collapsed behind me blocking the door through which I had entered.

By this time I was coughing so hard that I had to hold my breath at times. I had only one option, to go through the flames and exit with Xavier through the back window at the rear of his room. I grabbed a blanket from Xavier's bed and quickly wrapped him in it. Then I reached for a chair and hurled it through the window.

I knew if we were going to escape this inferno, I had only seconds left to do so. I held Xavier in my arms, and with a giant leap, I dove through the window. I found myself on the ground outside next to the house. I tried to get up and run, but I had apparently dislocated my hip when I landed on the ground. My instincts told me to crawl away from the hot fire, but I was still coughing very hard and so was Xavier Jr.

Just then a fireman swept us both up in his arms and carried us to safety.

We were still unable to talk, but soon we were breathing somewhat normally.

When I regained my sense of control, I asked Xavier if he was all right. He held out his arms and started to cry. I thought he was going to be okay, but he continued his crying and coughing.

As Xavier Jr. held out his left arm, I could see it was very red and badly burned. He started to cry again, and I gently picked him up being careful not to touch the badly burned area. I told him that we were okay now, but he was still coughing incessantly and crying.

All this time I was still not able to walk or apply my body weight to my left hip, even though I was standing. I was beginning to feel pain, and I knew the hip was either broken or dislocated. I asked the fire captain for a doctor to examine my leg and look at Xavier's arm. He told me that a doctor was coming right away.

When the doctor arrived, he examined Xavier. Then he told the fire captain to lay me on my back. He had two men hold my shoulders while he pulled hard on my leg. I felt a sharp pain as the hip snapped back into place. They helped me stand until the pain gradually subsided.

The doctor told me to take Xavier to the Burn Center in Saint Petersburg. As we arrived, we were greeted by Dr. Staskov, an expert on burns. He examined Xavier's arm and told me that he could treat him with herbs in order to heal the burn so that there would be no scars or damage to the muscle. I was thankful for that.

After two weeks of treatment, Xavier Jr. was released, and we were allowed to return home. I went to the home of my boss, Mr. Yorginov, where he greeted us with open arms. He found out that we had survived the fire, and he was very happy. He insisted that we move in with his family. He told me that he had opened a new bakery shop close to his home and that Xavier Jr. and I were welcome to stay with him and his wife.

XAVIER

Just as we were about to leave Dimitrio's, Ejon came strolling in wearing his Swiss-Alpine clothes and displaying a big grin. He had received my letter in Movorka and came quickly.

He said, "Fancy meeting you here. Guess what I have for you? Yes, I have the money for you, that you gave me for safekeeping, plus $68.32 that the bank paid as interest. I have it all, as you requested."

The timing was perfect as I had five dollars and Anna had only three. I offered to pay him two hundred dollars for his services, but he declined. I insisted, and he finally agreed to take one hundred dollar for his fee. This left me with $2,168.32, which was far more than we needed for the wedding, our passage to the United States, and plenty to spare.

WEDDING

Ejon asked, "When is the wedding? I will be best man, yes?"

I was quick to agree, and Ejon gave both of us a warm hug and offered his congratulations.

I had a bit of a problem. The only clothes I had were a priest's robe and collar, and priests don't marry. We then went shopping and bought some new clothes for everyone.

Ejon had friends that owned a large restaurant and winery in Amorsk called Bacicova's, where they often held weddings. He arranged for the wedding and reception there. Anna's boss furnished a grand cake and joined us all for the ceremony and dinner. The restaurant owner, who arranged for the music and the ceremony, also joined us for dinner. I wasn't sure, but I thought Ejon, paid for the feast, as they told us there was no charge. They sent us home in a four-horse carriage belonging to Bacicova's. Oh, how exciting this all was!

This long-awaited union between Anna and I was a night of magic that left the two of us undeniably fulfilled. We had dreamed about our wedding for a long time, and I was indisputably the happiest man in the world that night, thanks to God and my family. My patience had paid off, and those many nights in Ivan's prison were now only a faint glimmer in my memory.

We bid farewell to Ejon, a friend without whom we could never have accomplished all this and a friend that we would be truly grateful to for years to come. We thanked him for all he had done for us and wished him the best for the future as we bid farewell.

We boarded a train bound for Germany, where we could get Anna's and Xavier Jr.'s visas for immigration.

While all this was happening, Michael was in Berlin searching for his fiancée, Sonya. His efforts had not paid off as yet, but he was driven by his unyielding love for her that grew more intense by the day.

CHAPTER X
MICHAEL
MICHAEL'S SEARCH FOR SONJA

I figured that Sonja must have gone back to Berlin; that was where we planned to marry. She could possibly be there right now waiting for me. I knew one thing for sure: she wasn't any place in Russia.

Berlin was hundreds of miles away, and it took me several days by train to get there. My search started by going directly to the last known address of Peter Koonz. As I stood in front of 357 Abel Strassen, my heart was pounding, and my face was flushed with emotion. It was 6:30 a.m., and I thought maybe I should wait until later, possibly until 8:00 a.m. My waiting was short-lived as the front door sprang open and an elderly lady briskly stepped forth.

"Hi," I offered. "My name is Michael Roth, and I'm looking for Peter Koonz. Is this his residence?"

The response was not at all what I had wanted to hear. She gave me a suspicious glare, as she said, "Nine, he moved to Frankfurt about a year ago.

"Did he leave a forwarding address?" "Nine, I know of no such address."

"I desperately need to contact him. Is there anyone who can help me?"

"I have a letter that came a few months ago for him, but I don't know where to send it. Please wait a moment."

She was gone only minutes, and upon her return, she handed me the letter. I peered at it and could see that it was indeed from Sonja. I quickly suggested that I should take the letter to Peter when I locate him, of which she was most agreeable. I declined to open the letter because she might not understand.

She commented, "Peter has since moved from Frankfurt to New York City, but I can't help you there either."

I politely thanked her and was about to leave when the thought occurred to me.

Did Peter have any friends that might know where I can reach him? I didn't expect her to know, but she surprised me.

"Yes, his favorite spot was the Tarrinostra Club, just four blocks south of here, in that direction."

She pointed to her left, put her hands on her hips, and paused for a moment in a gesture indicating that she was through.

I quickly gave a nod and said, "*Danke.*"

"Just ask for Isabella, she sings and dances there."

Soon I found myself sipping a cold beer as I tore open the letter that the old lady had given me. My hands were trembling, and I had to lay it on the table to read it:

My Dear Peter,

I can't believe that you have not answered any of my letters. It is practically a matter of life or death for me, but still I get no help from you. You don't seem to give a damn. Perhaps you've met with foul play or have come down with some incurable disease; I pray not.

I desperately need to contact you as soon as possible. My fiancé, Michael Roth, has most likely sent you letters in search of me as he is equally desperate to locate me. Please help!

Michael and I plan to wed in Berlin as soon as he is released from the Cossacks, but since Bernhardt's death, we have lost contact with each other. You are the only one who can reunite us.

Please, if you have it in your power to help us, I beg you, do so at once.

Sincerely,
Sonja

PS: My current address is my place of employment. Please send all my mail to this address:

Books-Back to Back
1692 S. Market Strassen
Berlin, Germany

Sincerely,
Cousin Isabella

I managed a sigh of relief as I placed the letter back in my pocket, convinced that I had found her at last. I would go there and see her in the morning as the store is quite far away and would be closing in one hour.

MICHAEL MEETS A NEW FRIEND

I then asked the bartender if Isabella was working today, and he told me that she was. He then mentioned that she would start in about an hour. I finished my drink and leaned back to relax for a moment when she walked through the door. Her grace and charm was that of a princess, and I knew right away that she was someone special. I asked, "Would you be Isabella, my fair lady?" She hesitantly replied, "It is possible, and to whom do I owe this honor, my good man?"

"I go by the name of Michael, and I would be deeply in your debt if I might have a word with you, if you please."

She smiled and nodded, gesturing approval as I begin to explain my dilemma. She willingly gave me the particulars about Peter Koonz, telling me that they were cousins and that he now lived in New York City, but she hadn't heard from him for about six months.

"Would it be possible," I asked, "to get his address?"

She reached into her purse and muttered, "It's possible that he is still at this address."

She handed me a small slip of paper which read, 794 N. Queen St., New York, New York, USA.

I could see that she was wearing no wedding ring, and I became somewhat spellbound with this vivacious, extremely gorgeous woman.

"Thanks," I offered as she softly smiled. "Not at all. I'm happy I could help."

She was becoming noticeably flirtatious, which was extremely exciting to me. After all, I had been in battle for over five and a half years, and during that time had been deprived the company of a beautiful woman entirely.

I asked, "Do you work here?"

"Yes, I entertain. I sing and dance here. If you can stay for a while, you could catch my act."

I smiled and politely insisted, "Yes, I'd love to, my dear. Are you from out of town?"

"Yes, I'm from Madrid. You might have noticed my accent."

"Yes, it's extremely fascinating."

"Oh, how nice of you, Michael, how very nice of you to notice. I usually perform at the International Opera House through the summer, but we don't start there for ten more weeks. Sometimes I go home in the winter months, but then I do enjoy entertaining very much. My father will not allow me to sing and dance in my native country. He says it's not dignified for his daughter.

"I came to Germany to study musical theater as a very young girl, that's when I learned to speak German as well."

Then she asked, "Do you sing, Michael?"

"Oh yes, but only for the pigs and chickens as they seem to enjoy it so much. I'm convinced that those at the Opera House would not appreciate me very much."

She laughed and agreed, "Probably not."

As the evening continued, I could see that Isabella was very popular. Everyone knew her and stopped by our table to say hello. I was very flattered as she introduced me to her friends.

She would say, "This is my good friend, Michael Roth."

Just to be in her company was a thrill that gave my self-esteem a tremendous jolt. She was so pleasant and attentive like no one I had ever known.

I mentioned to her that I had just come from Russia and that I could use some work doing most anything.

She said, "Maybe I can help. Please stay, and we'll talk some more." "Thank you, I will. You have my word."

As the spotlight focused on her long flowing ebony hair, I was absolutely infatuated. This tall, slim Spanish beauty had captured my very being. The music started, and her sexy, sultry voice echoed through my brain like ripples on the water. As she slithered across the stage, my fantasies were running wild. At that moment I was completely captivated; I was a prisoner of my own imagination.

After her show, I complimented her on her flawless performance and told her that I loved her voice and dancing. She smiled and thanked me, and then she asked, "Do you have a place to stay tonight, Michael? I know you've been traveling."

I shrugged my shoulders and gave a bashful smile. She said, "Would you like to be my guest? I have plenty of room at my place."

A smile from me was all she needed, and I was eternally grateful.

Her place was profusely decorated with lavish tapestries and large paintings, which I assumed were from Spain. The furnishings looked like they had come from an old Spanish castle. They gave off an aura of nobility that told me they were custom-made for someone special.

After she poured two glasses of fine wine, she broke the silence. "Michael, I'm attracted to tall, handsome men, and you are so tall and strong, and so very handsome. Michael, do you mind?"

The question needed no answer, and I found myself reaching for her. I placed a gentle kiss on her hand, and as I pulled away, she ran her long delicate fingers through my hair and ended with a soft kiss on my lips. Isabella was so exciting that I nearly lost control.

MICHAEL'S INFATUATION

I'm here to find Sonja. What am I doing? I asked myself. What if I never find her? Life must go on!

We had one more glass of the delightful wine, and I dozed off. She gently covered me and kissed my forehead as she whispered softly with her beautiful accent, *"Buenas noches, mi amigo."*

I knew nothing of this language she spoke, but her accent had me spellbound.

I awoke to the aroma of food and hot coffee. Was I in heaven or just dreaming?

As we enjoyed our delicious breakfast, she asked, "Did you sleep well?"

"Yes, I did, really well."

"Why do you look for Peter Koonz? He's no good, and you are not like him at all, Michael."

I stammered for a moment, and then I explained,

"He was supposed to do me a favor and tell me where I might locate a friend, but he never answered my letters."

"Is this friend your wife or your lover?"

"Well yes, she's my fiancée and we plan to marry one day, but I haven't been able to locate her for quite some time."

"Does this mean that you are not available to me at this time?"

"Well, I'm not exactly sure.

"Maybe I can help you decide, Michael. Would you like that?"

I couldn't speak. I was already torn between Isabella, here in the flesh and blood, and Sonja, my lost love. I might never find Sonja again, and even if I did, would she be waiting for me? It's possible that she's met someone else, I told myself.

I had the answer delivered to me in a few glorious seconds. Isabella was devouring me with kisses, kisses like I'd never known in my entire life.

After this romantic time with Isabella, I knew what I had to do. I had to go to the bookstore where Sonja worked, talk to her in person, and see what was happening in her world.

I tried my best to explain to Isabella just what my thoughts were. I wanted to tell her exactly how I felt about her and what my intentions were concerning Sonja, but it was difficult.

She begged me to stay, to forget about Sonja, but my previous commitment to Sonja was the one that I felt most drawn to. I must go to the bookstore to see if Sonja still worked there and find out about her situation. Was Sonja still single, or was she unavailable to marry me as we once had planned? I honestly could not make a choice between these two beautiful women, at least not before finding Sonja and talking to her.

When I departed for the bookstore, I promised to return with my final decision in a few days. I found the bookstore where Sonja had been employed only a few short months earlier. I searched for Sonja inside the store, but she was not working.

I asked, "Is Sonja still working here?"

"No, not any longer. She quit, but she didn't say why and didn't tell anyone where she was going."

I was back to square one as Sonja had vanished again. At least I knew that she had been in Berlin and probably was still here somewhere.

MICHAEL'S STORY

I returned to Isabella's house to get the photo of Sonja, and I headed to Saint Christopher's Cathedral. I wanted to show it around again, hoping for a possible identification. No one seemed to know who she was or had ever heard of her. I left a photo with Mother Alicia and told her I would return soon.

Then I went back to Isabella's place. She was thrilled to see me and insisted that I stay with her for as long as I wanted. Our friendship grew, and I found myself so immensely fond of her that I suspected it was love. Isabella would attend mass at the cathedral on Sundays, but I usually stayed home. One Sunday she invited me to go with her; she offered a convincing smile, so how could I refuse her? As we entered the church, I noticed a small group of nuns welcoming parishioners. One nun stared at me as I sat down. She immediately came over to me.

MICHAEL FINDS SONJA

"Are you Michael Roth?"

When I heard her voice, I knew who she was, and I was speechless.

Then I blurted out, "Sonja, is that you?"

She only smiled and returned to the other nuns.

My mind drifted back to those days in the hospital in Movorka. By now I had no doubt in my mind. I was sure that this woman was Sonja, my long-lost lover, and now she was a nun—a nun! How could I ever expect to marry her now? She was a nun and dedicated to God and to the church. She could never marry anyone now.

As I glanced at Isabella, she was looking at me with a puzzled expression as if she were in a daze.

She asked, "Do you know this nun, Michael?"

I smiled and gave a huge sigh of relief because I knew my dilemma of selecting a bride had just been resolved.

Isabella had heard me speak to Sonja and knew quite well that this one-time rival was no longer a threat. She hesitantly repeated, "M-M- Michael?"

I quickly responded, "Isabella, will you marry me?"

Instead of a reply, she instantly took my hand and led me out the front door while I was proposing to her. She couldn't stop hugging and kissing me right there on the front steps of the cathedral. I was overcome with joy on one hand but stricken with sadness on the other. I loved Isabella with all my heart, but I also loved Sonja and had planned to marry her for nearly two years.

CHAPTER XI
MICHAEL
FUTURE PLANS

With much excitement in her voice, Isabella said, "We will be married in Spain at my family's home, yes?" I could not believe the way I felt; it was like being unearthed from a grave. I answered, "Yes, oh yes, if that would please you, my dear."

On Monday, I went back to the cathedral and asked for Sonja; she quickly appeared. The ease of her manner, which showed no signs of emotion, stunned me.

"Hello, Michael, how are you?"

"Sonja," I said, "I had to go to Germany, to get my expired visa renewed, but I was not permitted to return to Russia because my visa was to America only. I think that the Russian government was angry with me for leaving the Cossacks to move to America. However, I tried numerous times to contact you by mail with no response. I looked for you everywhere for months and months in the Berlin area, and finally I gave up all hope of ever finding you. Now that I have found you, I see that I'm too late."

"Yes, I know, Michael. I too tried to find you when I was released from the People's Will. After constantly checking with the cathedral hoping to find you, I finally asked the nuns for a job. I explained my dilemma to them, and they agreed to hire me to be in charge of their library. They offered me room and board and twenty dollars per month.

I figured that I could stay at the cathedral and look for you, and at the same time I was hoping and praying that you would show up.

"One day, God spoke to me about going into the convent. I had found much comfort in this new way of life and wanted to become a nun."

"Sonja, I did look for you, constantly. After Bernhardt died from the heart attack, I received a letter from his nephew, Peter Koonz. He informed me of Bernhardt's passing, and I was worried that he would not continue to correspond with either of us. Up until now, he has never responded to any of my letters, and now he's gone to New York City. Please forgive me. You were nowhere to be found. I even came here to the cathedral several times to show everyone your picture, but no one recognized you or your name."

"I was in the convent but was not well-known. They called me by my middle name, Marie, as it was more biblical sounding, so they didn't recognize the name Sonja. I didn't know it, but there were no visitors allowed until after graduation."

We said our reluctant goodbyes, and then we parted. And so it was that Sister Sonja was out of my life forever so it would seem. We can't know what fate has in store for us or what God's eternal plan might be, but my sincere desire to make Sonja my wife was snatched away from me in an instant.

I wondered how Xavier was doing in his search for Anna. I supposed that he had found her by now and that they were on their way to join Mom and Dad in South Dakota.

Isabella set a date for the wedding and plans were made for our trip to Spain. We had little time to ready ourselves now that we were engaged, and excitement seemed to capture the moment.

I spoke to Isabella about a pet name that I wanted to call her in private. She loved it; so it was official. "I would call her Izzy."

A knock on the door startled us both, and Izzy was quick to respond. As she opened the door, she was greeted by a priest and a nun from the cathedral.

The nun said, "We are here to ask for your attendance at Mass on Sundays." It wasn't until after she spoke that I realized it was Sister Sonja to whom Izzy was speaking.

Izzy replied, "I'm sorry. I promise to do better after the wedding." Sonja asked, "You are getting married?"

Complete silence settled over the room until I responded, "Yes, Isabella and I are to be wed at her family's home in Spain in one month."

Sonja stared at the floor, and I could feel that she was very uneasy with this conversation. Then I noticed a tear running down her cheek.

I was filled with sadness. After all that Sonja and I had been through and all her devotion and kindness to me, I felt that I had let her down somehow. She had been there for me and helped nurse me back to health from a very serious injury, and she had taught me the real meaning of love. I had so much to thank her for, but now I could only feel remorse and a gnawing sense of guilt.

Even though God surely willed that Sonja join his service, I knew that she had made this choice of her own free will. Yet I couldn't help but feel that I had abandoned her, and I prayed that she would eventually be okay with the way our romance had ended.

A few days later I received a note from Sonja apologizing, saying that she didn't know that I lived with Isabella. She was simply doing routine visits to parishioners, and she asked for my forgiveness.

She continued, "I can only say that I wish it were me you were to wed. I still love you with all my heart, but God has spoken."

Sonja found out where I was working and came by with a gift. I didn't know what to say, and I felt so sorry for her. We talked, and then she softly kissed my cheek. I quickly found myself holding her in my arms. She was my first real love, and I still had strong feelings for her.

As I released her, she kissed my lips ever so softly. I was instantly aroused, remembering those intimate times we shared back in Movorka. I struggled with my emotions and then we kissed with the utmost fervor.

I whispered, "Are you okay, my dear?

"No, no I'm not, but I will pray that God will ease my pain."

We quickly parted, but the tears that we both shed were a silent testament to the eternal love between us.

DEPART FOR SPAIN

As Isabella and I departed for Spain, I noticed something peculiar, and I asked her, "Who are these men that keep hanging around us? I believe they want something." These men were dressed in black and looked to be Spanish.

She replied, "Stay close beside me, Michael. I think they are bad men."

I asked Isabella again, "Who are these men that keep following us?

They are up to something, I believe."

Suddenly the two men rushed us, and they tried to take Isabella. I quickly jumped their horses, knocking one man off his horse, who then ran away while I held the other one and called for the police. They arrested the stalker and called Isabella by name, which I thought was unusual.

I asked Izzy, "What was that all about?"

"My father is in politics and has some enemies in Spain." "Can you get help from him? I am worried!" "Yes, I'll try."

Just then the police offered an escort to the border of France. I agreed, but I asked Isabella to arrange an escort for us through her father from the French border to Madrid.

I went to the store and bought two pistols to carry with us for protection. Izzy sent a telegram to her father requesting he meet us at the French border with a guard patrol. I figured this would keep us safe from harm.

ISABELLA KIDNAPPED

We spent the night in safety under the guard of the local police. At dawn we all got back on the road. Four armed guards from the local sheriff's office had been assigned to escort us to the border of France. Around noon we found an area to rest the horses and eat some lunch.

As we were about to leave, I noticed that the guards started acting nervous for some reason. They kept looking around as if someone were coming. Suddenly they all mounted their horses and rode away, back toward Stuttgart, the direction from which we had come.

I said, "Let's get out of here quickly. This looks like an ambush."

Just as I spoke, about ten or twelve Spaniards emerged, brandishing pistols.

We were completely unable to run as they had us surrounded.

One man held a gun to my head while the others bound and gagged Isabella. Then they bound me and tied me to a tree alongside the road. They told me that when I got free to go back to the Necar

River Inn, in the Black Forest. I would need to register under the name of Peter Lamendt and wait for further instructions.

I remembered passing the inn earlier that morning, and it was about one hours ride back toward Stuttgart. All I had to do was get loose or wait for someone to come along and untie me. I kept trying to loosen my ropes to no avail, and my fingers were bleeding from pulling on the knots.

Suddenly I heard a wagon coming my way, and I started yelling. A farmer who was going to Stuttgart with a load of pigs for the market heard me and stopped to see what the problem was. He cut the ropes to free me and asked if I were all right. I told him my story, and he said that the Black Forest had many robbers; one must be extremely careful! Our horses were still tied close by, so I drove our carriage and followed behind the farmer. We headed for the inn, and I prayed all the way. I thought about the guards that had set us up for this ambush, as they must have been paid off by the police before we left Stuttgart.

I registered at the inn as the kidnappers had demanded. A message was delivered to my room in about four hours. The envelope contained this message:

Peter Lamendt,

This is a ransom demand for one million dollars. We have also given this demand to Isabella's father. He has agreed to have the money delivered to you in Stuttgart on Friday. You, in turn, will deliver the money to me on Saturday. Wait for further instructions at the Palace Hotel in Stuttgart. Remember, Isabella's life depends entirely upon your cooperation.

Z

I made haste for the Palace Hotel in Stuttgart. As I traveled, I thought of Isabella's safety as well as my own. Once I had delivered the money, I was of no further use to these banditos and neither was Isabella. They could kill us both and still have the money. This was probably their plan, and I could not allow this to happen.

What options do I have? I asked myself.

The first person who came to mind was my brother Xavier. Where was he?

Was there any chance that I could get him here in time?

I quickly sent a telegram to the Swiss Underground asking them to locate Ejon Vogel and to have him contact me immediately at the Palace Hotel in Stuttgart. I explained that I needed the exact location of my brother Xavier and his destination.

Only six hours later, I received a reply from Ejon. He explained that Xavier and Anna would be arriving at the border town of Dresden, Germany, on Thursday, at 10:40 a.m., December 10, 1899.

XAVIER

After four days travel, we arrived at Dresden on the German border. We were returning to Germany, our home country, for Anna's visa to America. As we passed through Immigration, I was surprised to have a telegram waiting for me. I thought there must be a serious emergency in my family, for who else knew we were on this train? Only Ejon, I surmised. My hands were trembling as I opened the telegram. It read:

To: Xavier Roth, Dec. 10, 1899
Dear Brother Xavier,

I have encountered a situation where I am desperately in need of your help. Stop. Isabella, my loving wife to be, has been kidnapped near the town of Stuttgart, Germany, by some Spanish underworld banditos. Stop. They want one million dollars ransom. Stop. Isabella's father has sent me the money for delivery. Stop.

Train tickets await you at Bern Station where you are arriving near the border. Stop. Bring help and your Cossack weapons. Stop. I have two fast horses and plenty of backup. Stop.
A man named Bill King will be there to meet your train in Stuttgart. Stop.
I will explain the details when we meet on Friday night. Stop. Thank you, Xavier.

Love,
Brother, Michael

I quickly handed the message to Anna to read, and I waited for her response.

Who is this Isabella that Michael speaks of?

Mom told me about her when I was home last. She said that Sonja, Michael's previous fiancée, has become a nun and can't marry anyone now. Since then, Michael has met and is now engaged to a wonderful Spanish girl by the name of Isabella. That's all I know, except that she is very beautiful and talented and that she speaks four languages. She also seems to have lots of money, so I'm told.

"Isabella? Isn't that the name of the Queen of Spain?" "Yes, Anna, I do believe so."

"Do you think—?" she blurted out.

We quickly retrieved our luggage and transferred it onto the train going south to Stuttgart. As I gathered my thoughts, I asked the conductor how long it took to get to Stuttgart. He replied, "Its only a day and a few hours from here, about twenty-six hours altogether."

We had only been moving for a few minutes when I noticed a very tall man sitting about six rows in front of me. The shape of his head looked familiar, and as he turned to talk to someone, I was shocked to see that it was indeed, Ivan Vasalov, my Cossack comrade and my student of religion. I jumped out of my seat, and I was standing beside Ivan in seconds. He was shocked to see me, and we exchanged greetings.

I asked, "Ivan, what are you doing here?"

"My wife is from Stuttgart, and we are on our way to visit her parents.

We were just married on December 1, only ten days ago." "Congratulations!" I energetically exclaimed as I shook his hand. "I repeated my well wishes once again as I looked over at his bride of ten days and gently shook her hand."

I told him that Anna and I had been married only four days. Then I beckoned Anna and Xavier Jr. to come and meet Ivan and his wife. I introduced them as my friends, Mr. and Mrs. Vasalov, and added that Ivan and I had fought together in the Cossacks which made us comrades forever. Anna didn't know of my time in Ivan's prison nor was I about to expose her to that aspect of our relationship at this time.

I explained to Ivan that my brother Michael was in Stuttgart, and his fiancée had been kidnapped by some Spaniards who were holding her for a one million-dollar ransom. I told him that I was on my way there to help get her back and to protect her and Michael during the money exchange.

"I have my Cossack weapons and boots along with me, and I need some help."

I paused for a moment; I then asked, "Ivan, wouldn't it be spectacular if you and I were to team up together on this? We could protect the girl and recover the money." I slowly added, "There's a big reward if we can pull it off. You can take some time to think it over if you'd like."

Ivan explained the situation to his wife and gave her some time to answer. She quickly responded, "Your comrades are in need of your help, Ivan, and they would do the same for you if you needed them. It's good to help your brothers. I say yes, my husband, go and help them."

Ivan smiled as he nodded his head.

"I too have my Cossack weapons and boots with me, and I would consider it a privilege to ride by your side, my brother."

When we arrived in Stuttgart, we were met by Michael's man, Bill King. I introduced him to Ivan, and then we were escorted to lunch where Bill explained the plan to us. He then took us to the Mission of the Pines where he introduced us to his wife, Estrella, who was to provide care for us while the rescue took place.

Bill handed me a letter from Michael, which I quickly opened:

Dear Xavier,

You are indeed a magnificent brother. I can't tell you how much it means to me just having you by my side at this difficult time. I'm sure that you understand. I hope you will be able to find another confidant to work with us on this very delicate mission.

Bill King will bring you to my hiding place at 6:00 p.m. tonight. We will put together a plan for tomorrow, which will take your vast experience and know-how to initiate. The counterattack will be very critical, and the timing will play a huge part in our success, as you know.

Bill is a retired Austrian border patrol leader and comes highly recommended. He is, above all, a completely trustworthy professional. He has a group of subordinates to cover the less critical aspects of the rescue and to protect the money while it is in my possession.

I was able to find you through the Swiss Underground. Ejon Vogel knew the time and date of your departure and your arrival time in Dresden.

Isabella's father is sending one million dollars for ransom. I'm sure we can get it back, aren't you?

Your grateful brother,
Michael

Just as we finished dinner, I saw Bill approaching, and I had my Cossack clothes and weapons ready and waiting for the next move. I explained to Bill that Ivan and I had been Cossacks together in many battles and that he was here at Michael's request to ensure the safety and protection of Isabella. I requested one more fast horse for Ivan, along with the two we had already secured.

We came to the mission the back way, so as not to attract attention, and we waited until Michael arrived.

MICHAEL

I said to my team, "Good, I see everyone is here, and the plan will soon be implemented. Ivan, I'm excited that you have agreed to be a big part of our team. I welcome your knowledge and experience. We need you and Xavier to speak out whenever you have something to add, agreed?"

"Yes," they both replied.

"I am to deliver the money to them tomorrow at noon. They want it delivered in a metal box to a destination that is unknown at this time. I'm to go to the school for the blind and wait at the base of the bell. The school is about one mile north of town on Zentrum Road.

"Someone will deliver instructions to me and give me directions from there.

I must act alone, or they will kill Isabella.

"We will need sentinels posted along the way on horseback, in every direction from the school, to allow us to keep track of the man with the money.

"The metal box that holds the ransom money will need a lighter gauge box attached to the back that will hold a noise-smoke bomb that is set on a timer. It will explode and attract attention but won't damage the money.

"The border guards will then converge on the noise and smoke area, and the Cossacks will make sure that Isabella is safe and try to recover the money."

XAVIER

"If there is not a clean release of Isabella, we will do whatever is necessary to protect her and bring her home safely."

IVAN

"We will be close by, but you won't see us. Trust me, we will cover your backs."

MICHAEL

"Okay," I interjected. "Is everyone in agreement?" They all replied with a unanimous yes.

Michael continued, "Bill, you will take care of the money box and the bomb tonight. Set the timer for 12:20 p.m. tomorrow. I will be here at 8:30 a.m. with the ransom money. Be ready!

"The border guards will converge on the scene and capture all the Spaniards. They will then turn them over to the German police for prosecution!" I commented, with much enthusiasm. "Between the guards and the Cossacks, we can't fail!"

"We think we know where their hideout is located right now, but it's too risky to rush the building as Isabella could be injured or killed. We have a man with binoculars watching around the clock who will notify us of any new developments," I reiterated.

"Above all, Isabella must be released at the exact same time the money is paid; she is priority number one. The capture of the money and its return is secondary.

"Bill is in charge of the border patrol personnel and will coordinate with me continuously. He has everything mapped out already as to his sentinels' strategic locations. Three shots at five-second intervals will alert everyone to converge on the scene.

"Xavier and Ivan are feared Cossack warriors that can bring down armies. They are here to guarantee our successful mission along with myself, who holds the same qualifications.

"I will check out the girl that they surrender to make sure that she is the real Isabella."

After our quick strategy session, we were all set with every base covered. The bomb was set to detonate at 12:20 p.m., and my watch was synchronized with the clock. All we had to do was make it happen. We ensured that the bomb could be defused in a matter of seconds in case of a change in plans.

We found it difficult to sleep under these conditions, from the stress of it all. We were up at dawn and anxious to get rolling.

RESCUE OF ISABELLA

At 11:00 a.m., we were all in our places. The Cossack horses and weapons were set to go. The sentinels were distributed to cover all possible escape routes. I had the moneybox, and the bomb was ready to explode in eighty minutes, but I was still in our hideout. I gave my weapons to Xavier, who would have them for me if and when I needed them.

I was soon on my horse and headed for the blind school, which was closed on Saturdays. I had on my Cossack boots, but I refrained from tucking my pants inside to prevent giving myself away.

As I tied my horse to the base of the bell, I checked the time; it was now five minutes before noon. I held the box containing the bomb and the money and sat quietly next to the bell. I watched sharply while a man dressed in Spanish clothing came closer. He whistled, threw a package toward me, and then he quickly ran away. I picked up the package and removed the lid. I found this note inside:

Michael Roth,

You have followed instructions perfectly. Please continue to do what I say, and no one will get hurt.
You must take the money now, and don't talk to anyone. Go to the end of this road past the white house on the right, and then ride slowly for about 1/4 mile to the creek. I will be there with Isabella to make the trade.

Z

I figured that Bill King and his boys wouldn't be able to help me once I was out of their sight, and I didn't want to botch the swap. Of course Xavier and Ivan had their eye on me from somewhere. I had a small pistol hidden on my saddle, so I decided to slip it into my boot under my pants before heading to the creek. I wished I had my Cossack weapons to give me some protection, but I figured I couldn't conceal them anyway.

As I got to the end of the road, I noticed Xavier hidden under the branches of some large hickory trees, and I was glad to know that he had me covered. I was concerned about the noise bomb as it was set to go off in eleven minutes. I continued on for a few more minutes along the cattle trail and could see some small trees ahead, indicating that there was water.

I saw a movement in the bushes, and a voice called out, "Get down from your horse, and I'll bring the girl."

I quickly honored his wishes and stood beside my horse awaiting more directions. I heard Izzy say, "Michael, thank God you've come."

Then the Spaniard called out, "I will release her when the money is in my hands, but you must leave the money where you are and walk away fifty steps. If all the money is not there, I will be forced to have my sniper shoot the girl."

I replied, "If you harm the girl in any way, I promise I will hunt you down and feed your carcass to the buzzards."

The clock was still ticking in the moneybox, and I could see that there was less than two minutes left. As I sat the money box on the ground, I called out, "Here you are, one million dollars!"

As I led my horse away, I noticed that Mr. Z was not alone. He quickly walked toward the moneybox while his partner held on to Isabella. I yelled out, "Not so fast, you must release the girl!"

He laughingly replied, "What are your options, señor?"

He grabbed the box and ran back to where his partner held Izzy.

I checked my watch. There were only twenty seconds remaining. During all this commotion, Ivan had quietly walked his horse down the creek bed. I caught a glimpse of his horse, but Ivan was out of sight, waiting for my next move.

I hollered, "Run, Izzy! Run fast!"

Both Spaniards were looking at the million dollars when the bomb went off. The blast knocked them both off their feet, so I instantly mounted my horse and snatched Isabella from the spot where she had run.

I saw a flash of Xavier as he charged the two men lying on the ground by the moneybox. By then Ivan had joined in, but several other Spaniards approached and were trying to pick up the money. The Cossack whips were in action, and I could hear the kidnappers screaming.

I sat Izzy down on the ground and rode to where Xavier and Ivan were fighting off six or eight Spaniards. Xavier handed me his lance, and we all confronted these banditos together. Ivan picked up the box, which still held most of the money while Xavier and I took care of the remaining Spaniards. Xavier whipped the guns from their hands while I ran my lance through several. They did not give up the money easily. Ivan protected the money while holding two wounded banditos at gunpoint. I fired the location shots to help the rest of our team find us. The border guards arrived in time to run down the remaining banditos while the rest of the Spaniards lay on the ground, either dead or wishing they were dead.

I returned to Isabella who had watched in horror as those ten Spaniards faced Ivan, Xavier, and me. Four were dead, and two more were injured badly. By this time, all the remaining Spaniards were in custody.

Isabella spoke out, "Michael, you saved my life, you, Xavier, and your friend. Thank you! Thank you! I love you forever!"

I held her tightly in my arms, reassuring her that she was safe now.

She was trembling and crying almost to the point of hysteria. "Izzy," I asked, "are you okay?"

She paused for a few seconds and replied, "What took you so long?" We each took a deep breath and held on to each other very tightly.

By this time the sound of the bomb had attracted the entire rescue squad together. After they heard the bomb explode, they followed the smoke cloud and the sound of the shots that I had fired.

The mission was completed, thanks to our Cossack training and three seasoned Cossack warriors. The money was all recovered, though some was a little charred. The ransom money was returned to Isabella's father who had just arrived on the scene. He insisted on giving a thousand dollars to everyone who took part in the rescue and ten-thousand to Xavier, Ivan, and Bill King, who played major roles. He also covered all of our expenses.

Above all, my precious Isabella was safe, although noticeably shaken. She was hugging Xavier, Ivan, and me all at the same time while she shed a few tears. Without Ivan's help, we would have had a difficult time. We stayed through the night with the protection of Bill King and his crew, but we were back on the road at dawn. This time we had six of the Austrian border patrol as escorts all the way to the border of Spain and France. From there to Izzy's home in Spain, we were protected by a troop of the Royal Spanish Guardsmen, furnished by the king.

A royal carriage and two white stallions, along with eight soldiers of the Royal Spanish Guard, were dispatched to bring the best man and his wife from Stuttgart to the wedding. It was said that, excluding the groom, the next "best man" at the wedding was seven-foot tall, Ivan Vasalov, and I didn't know anyone who wished to argue that point.

AUTHOR

Xavier and Anna had only a few days remaining to process through Immigration before the expiration of their visas to the

United States. They were on their way to join Simon and Ingrid, who had preceded them to South Dakota. Consequently, Xavier and Anna were unable to attend Michael and Isabella's wedding ceremony.

XAVIER'S DEPARTURE FOR AMERICA

Xavier and Anna boarded the train at Stuttgart and were bound for Brussels. After nearly two days they arrived at the seaport of Reise, where they were transported by small craft to the London Harbor. The USS, Ulysses S. Grant passenger liner was scheduled to depart for New York in just six hours. The trip was expected to take twenty-nine days. They anticipated arriving in New York on January 20, 1900, at 2:30

p.m. Since this was the stormy season on the Atlantic, they encountered some hurricane winds of over eighty miles per hour that impeded their progress. The ship had to change course at one point to avoid a powerful storm that would have been a danger to both the passengers and crew.

On their sixteenth day from London, Xavier Jr. came down with a high fever, and the ship's doctor was unable to help him. Days went by, and still he would not eat. He coughed incessantly and had trouble breathing.

Anna remembered what her mother had done for her when she was sick as a child. She asked the cook for some dry mustard and some towels. Then she made a mustard plaster and placed it on Xavier Jr.'s chest for a few hours.

In the morning his fever was gone, and he was hungry. After three more days, he was able to walk about the ship, and he was much better.

The doctor told Anna that he must have had pneumonia, but he was better now.

The change in course had added five days to their arrival time, but since they avoided the worst of the storm, they arrived late but safe in New York on January 25, 1900.

XAVIER

As we arrived in New York, the weather was freezing cold, with ten inches of new snow on the ground. The streets were impassable with snow and ice everywhere. Consequently, we had no way to travel about other than by foot.

I had the address of my uncle Edward in Aberdeen, South Dakota, so we decided to take the train directly to South Dakota. The next departure time was in five hours, which was shortly after midnight. This turned out to be perfect as it took three hours to get our luggage from the ship and to clear Customs and Immigration.

Grand Central Station was warm, and we were hungry, so we just spent some time relaxing over a nice hot meal.

Even though New York was snowbound, it still felt wonderful to be there. Our hopes and dreams had been realized, and the beginning of our new life in America was starting. We were all so delighted.

We sent a telegram from Grand Central Station to Uncle Edward before we boarded the train. We figured that he could tell Mom and Dad we were coming.

Soon we were on our way to join my parents. They should be settled in by now as they must have arrived in Aberdeen in early January, nearly a month ago. We wondered if Mom had delivered the baby yet, and we were anxious to see everyone.

All went well, and Xavier Jr. enjoyed the train ride. We arrived in Aberdeen on the morning of January 29. It was very cold, but no more ice and snow.

CHAPTER XII
MICHAEL
TRAVEL TO MADRID

The trip from Germany to Madrid took several days as we would rest at night and travel about nine to ten hours a day. There were many small hotels along the way and quaint restaurants with good Spanish food.

Many people recognized Isabella and called her by name. Since Izzy had traveled this route many times before, that could possibly explain her popularity. Of course, she might be royalty like I had originally suspected, but I told myself that was not likely. Only time would give the answers I sought. Regardless of the outcome, it really didn't matter as I loved her either way.

We were glad to finally arrive at Isabella's home. It appeared to be a giant palace with many other impressive buildings adjoining. By this time, I was convinced that Isabella was indeed royalty, a princess no doubt. Everything I had suspected appeared to be absolutely true.

I purposely showed no sign of surprise nor did I ever comment about such splendor. I figured I'd play Izzy's little game and be as nonchalant about it all as she was being.

Everyone was excitedly conversing with her and giving her what appeared to be hugs of congratulations. I only smiled as I shook hands with practically everyone, and I was trying hard to be as calm as I knew I was expected to be. I spoke, but her family was not bilingual. However, they were very cordial and supportive of Isabella.

I was overwhelmed with the "house," as Izzy called it. It was indeed a giant palace of the Royal Family. As I observed the entire estate, I discovered that some of the servants addressed Isabella as princess, and I began to see that she was indeed just that. Not wanting to make an issue of this, I merely accepted it all and figured that Isabella would discuss it with me in due time.

The place was like a bee's hive. Ivan and I were being fitted for formal Spanish suits, and Izzy was to wear her mother's wedding gown from nearly thirty years prior. I had little doubt that it would be exquisite.

People arrived from everywhere, and a parade was scheduled in our honor with soldiers and the Royal Spanish Marching Band. Cannons were fired along with fireworks and rockets, and the crowd cheered and cheered. Such a fabulous affair was this! The wealth and splendor were beyond my wildest imagination, and it was simply sensational. It far exceeding any fairy tale I had ever heard or read about.

The palace where Isabella was born and grew up was over five hundred years old and had withstood many wars. There were servants everywhere, and delicious food awaited us around the clock. I was thinking that the great food was fit for a king, which caused me to chuckle inwardly.

Izzy's accommodations were that of the visiting Royalty Quarters, lavish and spacious, as one might expect, with a formal garden just off the formal dining room. This, naturally, would be the honeymoon suite after the wedding. My quarters were simple, but I liked it that way. They far exceeded the barn where we'd lived on the Black Sea and would more than suffice for these few days until the wedding night.

Twelve hundred guests were expected to attend the ceremony, which left me in shock. What had I gotten myself involved in? Would this be my undoing? I inhaled an enormous gulp of air, and I held it for half a minute. As I exhaled, I playfully suggested to Isabella that we might need a larger place for the wedding.

She caught on instantly and spoke right out, "What about Buckingham Palace, my love?"

We laughed at the thought, and she bent over to where I sat.

As she kissed my cheek, she commented, "You know, it's too late to change your mind, Michael. There's no turning back."

My smile of approval dispelled any possibilities of that as I replied, "Perish the thought, my love."

My thoughts wandered, and I could not help myself.

I asked, "Why me, Isabella? Why did you choose me from the host of all the men in the world, when you could have anyone you chose?"

"Michael, you are the one, the one who was destined for me. I knew it the first time I laid eyes on you. Don't you agree, my love?"

"Absolutely, my dear," I humbly replied.

From that moment on, I never doubted that we would be inseparable for the rest of our lives.

Ivan and I were rushed into a small room where we discovered all of our wedding attire waiting. We had two assistants helping to get us ready, and all was going well. The formal suits and all were of the finest material I had ever seen, and everything fit perfectly.

Ivan thanked me for the honor of being chosen best man, and I assured him that the honor was all mine.

I wondered how my bride would look in her mother's gown; however, the wait was short-lived.

SPANISH WEDDING TO PRINCES ISABELLA

Soon the music started, and we were positioned in our places for the ceremony. I couldn't wait to see Isabella; my pulse was racing. I felt flush in the face as beads of perspiration formed on my brow.

I looked over my shoulder and back down the aisle of the garden where those beautiful flowers lined each side. I could see many of Isabella's friends starting to walk our way when all at once the music changed.

As everyone stood up, I looked back toward the entrance. Izzy and her father were slowly walking my way. Two small girls threw rose petals on the pathway in front of Isabella while two older boys carried the train of her gown. As she approached, she smiled and winked her flirtatious eye at me. I was completely intoxicated by her beauty.

Her gown was covered with precious gems and pearls, but she was the most precious gem of them all. She was radiant and sparkling as though made from the Crown Jewels. Her flowing black hair was like a sheet of silk, with a white flower resting over her left ear. She was adorned in a massive diamond necklace with matching earrings.

Her father was dressed in his formal royal garments, worn only by the king. I shall remember this patronage of royal magnitude until my dying day. He was uncontrollably beaming with pride, showing his obvious fondness for Isabella. He was tall and straight; his every step was sure and true.

I felt as if I were a prince or at least someone really special. Technically, I guess I would become a prince in just a few moments when the ceremony was concluded. I was the most important man in town even though I had not officially been granted the title of prince at that time.

The ceremony was in Spanish of course, and I was scared to death. I didn't understand one word that was spoken, but one thing I knew for sure, I was taking a bride, a beautiful bride, one that I loved completely.

Soon the ceremony was over, and then the fun began. I was introduced to all the royal family, Spanish Generals, many Spanish dignitaries, many important friends of the royal family, and leaders from many foreign countries. I smiled and said *gracias* (thank you) a lot. What else could I do?

After two-and-one-half hours of such fun, we were finally through with the introductions. I was exhausted and so was Isabella. We cut the cake, and everyone clapped and cheered. I was a married man, and I was a husband, an *esposo* as Izzy called me.

I couldn't let it go. I reflected back to Sonja, and even though we were finally able to bring our relationship to a close, I felt that I was somehow cheating her of a wedding and the love and devotion that marriage can bring. I felt my heart would burst. Oh God, I thought, how can I possibly forget her?

Then I realized that Izzy was there beside me, my wife, my lover, my dream come true, and my magical gift from God. This was evidently part of his eternal plan and who was I to question the wisdom of God?

The celebration continued through half the night, and finally we retired to our quarters where we shared a night of bliss and intense ecstasy, far beyond description.

After a morning of delightful food and wine, we walked hand in hand through the garden. Izzy spoke of spending a few days at her parent's beach house near Valencia. I was eager to vacate the palace and to be alone with my beautiful bride, the fabulous Isabella.

Valencia was an ancient and romantic seaport on the Mediterranean Sea, and it was a fabulous resort area. The water was crystal clear and reflected the blue from the sky. Our honeymoon cottage was situated on a peninsula with a delightfully private beach. Our excitement soared as we were finally alone, except for the servants, who came only when summoned.

The house was of Greek architecture and quite large. It had a huge pool and several fishponds that were surrounded by statues of Aquarius, mermaids, and dolphins. It was splendid and self-indulgent. The entrance was guarded by two huge, marble lions that appeared to be centuries old. Six tall marble pillars gave the appearance of the Parthenon, the Athenian temple of architectural fame from the fifth century.

It was, in simple words, quite extravagant, made to host large parties for special occasions. I was comfortable there, but one could easily get lost within its confines.

The spring weather was warm, and we strolled on the beach enjoying the scenery and the salty air. We had a small sailboat anchored at the dock, so we decided to go sailing. One of the caretakers, Pablo, was an experienced sailor, and Isabella had been sailing with him many times over the years.

We got out on the water early the next morning with the wind at about eighteen knots. We sailed up and down the shoreline, viewing the many splendid resorts on the beach. There were many other small crafts on the water, all doing the same.

It was my first trip on a sailboat, and I was fascinated with everything. The speed and the quiet of the sailboat was an experience I'd always remember. Pablo explained everything to Izzy in Spanish, which she translated for me, and soon I was sailing by myself. I figured that I could handle this small boat the next time we went sailing without the help of an instructor.

Isabella wanted to go shopping that afternoon, so we went to town. She said that her dad owned a nice store along the beach. Before the day was over, I was decked out in shorts, a bright shirt, and a new pair of zapatas (shoes). I could have passed for a local hombre. Izzy, of course, as a local señora, looked good in all Spanish clothing.

We finished up the day with a nice dinner at Señor Arturo's, and the floor show was quite nice. Then Isabella's presence was recognized in the house, and she was instantly invited to perform.

She had sung and danced there many times before with these local mariachis, and she was simply superb. I could only compare that night's performance with Izzy's Terrinostra Show in Berlin. It was amazing, and I knew I had just witnessed Isabella at her best, here at home in Spain, with a traditional Spanish band. She was sensational, a true superstar giving a rare performance that brought down the house.

I was bursting with pride as she graciously introduced me as Michael, the Prince of Spain. I stood to be recognized.

NEW HACIENDA

On the tenth day we returned to Madrid, and Izzy asked me, "Would you like to live in Spain, or should we go back to my little house in Berlin? We can always go to wherever you would like best. What is your choice, my love?"

"Isabella, as long as we are together, I would live anywhere."

She smiled overwhelmingly and replied, "Good! Then I will show you around and see if you like it here in Spain. Would you like to see our wedding gift from my mother and father?"

"Yes, I would like that very much, what is it?" "It's a beautiful house in our family vineyards."

I thought back to the house that Dad, my brothers, and I had built in Odessa on the Black Sea. I remembered how hard we had worked and what little money we had to build the house. Tears came to my eyes.

Izzy said, "What are your thoughts, Michael? You do not like the idea too much?"

I cleared my throat and found myself speechless at such generosity. I finally managed some words.

"Isabella, my love, you and your family are now my family, and I can only find love and peace in my heart for such kind and loving people. You, my dear, are absolutely the most kind and loving of all. What can I say? I know I'll love the house, and I thank your parents for such a generous wedding gift."

We departed the next morning to go see the house that Izzy had told me about, the one she loved so very much. I could see in her eyes that this house was special to her, and I knew that I would love it too. We enjoyed the trip and took in the sights along the way. As we traveled through the many vineyards and small villages, I spotted a beautiful hacienda with many buildings.

"Isabella, look at that beautiful hacienda."

"Yes, Michael, it is ours if you like it. It's our wonderful wedding gift from my parents."

I closed my eyes and tried to comprehend that this was not a dream. How could this be happening to me, a common German farmer, a Cossack, and a very poor man? As we stopped in front of the house, I could see that it was made of huge stones. It was much larger than I had envisioned in my mind, and my heart nearly stopped when I saw it. Only three months earlier, I was looking for a place to spend the night when Isabella invited me to her home in Berlin.

"Do you like it, Michael? What do you think, my love?" "It's wonderful! This is our house, Izzy? Can we go inside?"

The front door was about fourteen-foot high and made of heavy mahogany with large iron hinges. It was like the ones I made for our front door in Odessa. The rooms, about twenty-five in all, were about fourteen-foot tall. The walls were adorned with many large paintings and more tapestry. It was rustic yet elegant, with Spanish antiques throughout.

"Come and see our bedroom, Michael. I hope you like it."

The bedroom was carpeted with the most exquisite, ornate Persian rugs I'd ever seen. The bed was massive with brass monkeys at the corners and a canopy cover over the top. The bedspread was a thick, fluffy goose-down quilt. The rest of the furnishings were spectacular as well, like the ones in Izzie's house in Berlin.

A large painting of a king hung above the headboard. I inquired, "Who is the man in the painting?"

"That's my papa, my grandfather, King Ferdinand, from many generations back."

"Ah yes, you are a princess, just like I suspected when I first met you." She only smiled, "Do you mind, Michael?" "Not at all, my love. I think it's fascinating."

I didn't begin to comprehend the magnitude of her royalty as I was only a simple man.

"Do you like it so far, Michael?"

"Yes, it's fabulous. It's the most beautiful house I've ever seen." "There is more to see, Michael."

She continued to guide me through the house, and just as I thought we were through with the tour, she started out the side door. She asked, "Would you like to see more?"

"There's more?" I inquired.

She took my hand and escorted me to a large building about 250 feet behind the house. Several smaller shops with about ten large tanks adjoined them.

Over the door of the largest building was a sign that read Isabella III. I hesitantly asked, "Is this your winery?" She smiled and answered, "It's 'our' winery, my love, yours and mine.

"Is there an Isabella I and II also?"

"Of course, how else could there be an Isabella III, silly?"

Again I closed my eyes and shook my head in disbelief, wondering just how many more surprises Izzy still had for me. My beautiful Isabella was a lot deeper than I had ever imagined. She was complex yet so simple in many ways. She was so loving and giving, and I was such a lucky man, the winner of the grand prize.

As we entered the winery, we were approached by the Master Winemaker, an elderly gentleman who greeted us.

"*Buen dia,* Isabella." (Good day, Isabella.) "Yo te felicito." (I congratulate you.)

"He was telling us congratulations on our marriage,"

Izzy quickly replied, *"Mucho gracious, Pedro."* (Thank you very much, Pedro.)

"El es mi esposo, Michael." (This is my husband, Michael.) Pedro responded, *"Mucho gusto, señor."* (Happy to meet you, sir.)

Izzy continued to converse with the old man, and soon we were riding in a cart pulled by a burro through the largest building. She explained much of the process of winemaking to me; it was fascinating.

I asked, "Do we get a sample of the wine?"

"It's now only grape juice, but we can have wine when we go to the cellar later on. It takes a few years to age the wine for the best flavor, my love. We will soon sample many of the vintage wines that you will love."

As we returned to the house, Izzy asked, "Michael, can we move here and make this our home?"

What was I to say to all of this, a fabulously beautiful wife, a spectacular home, three wineries, and a ready-made royal family? Yes, I was sure I must be dreaming. Those were my thoughts as I responded,

"If it makes you happy, then yes, I will agree." "Oh, Michael, you are so very kind to me."

As she spoke those words, I wanted to say that she was the kind one for sharing all this with me, but I declined to comment and simply reveled in her praise.

The very next day, Isabella ordered our house to be cleaned and made ready for us. There was all new bedding, and everything was dusted and polished. Fresh flowers filled the vases, and there was a pantry full of delicious foods.

Izzy said, "In three days, we will come to our new home to live. Is this okay, my husband?"

I hugged and kissed her, and she quickly had her answer. I was happy to be leaving the palace because it was much too formal and much too busy for a farm boy, especially one who had once lived in a barn. I was also anxious to learn more about winemaking and growing grapes; after all, I was a farmer, and I knew how to make crops grow. I was filled with excitement and anticipation, and I was also ready to be alone with my charming new bride, the former princess, and now my queen.

CHAPTER XIII
XAVIER
ARRIVING IN SOUTH DAKOTA

Mom and Dad had been notified that we were on our way, and they were anxious to see us and meet Anna and Xavier Jr. Everyone was waiting at the train station, and we had a grand welcome. Dad was expecting to see a little boy with us since Xavier Jr. was only three years old, but the boy was so tall that he looked to be much older. Mom and Anna made friends instantly, and Dad would not leave his grandson alone. Anna baked bread and rolls, Russian-style, and everyone loved them. Olga was now over two months old, and she was cuddly and cute and looked like Mom. I could see that she was Mom's long-awaited prize after bringing up so many boys. Lambert worked for a large wheat farmer and lived there with his family; it was only eight miles to Mom and Dad's place.

He was still troubled from the stress of the battlefield and couldn't let it go. He would hallucinate often and would sometimes wake up screaming from the nightmares that he suffered as a result of his years in the Cossacks. He slept in the barn most of the time, fearful that he might wake up and accidentally hurt someone.

Anna, Xavier Jr., and I went to live with Mom and Dad, who had just settled into their new farm. I had the money that I had been paid for the rescue of Isabella, which was enough to buy a section of prime wheat land.

I wasn't sure that I wanted to go back into farming at this time. I remember being fascinated when Dad built the house on the Black Sea, and I felt drawn to the building trade as a way to support my family. I finally rented a house in town, and after getting better acquainted, I took a job with a construction company.

Soon I started to contract on my own as I really liked this sort of work. I built the first schoolhouse in town and the first church. I built a fine home for Anna and Xavier Jr. next to the school. It wasn't long before I had more work than I could possibly do, so I increased the size of my construction company. I was soon building all over North and South Dakota.

TORNADO

The weather was often unpredictable in the spring and throughout the summer. Sometimes we would get warnings of tornadoes headed our way. One evening, when we had just finished our dinner, we heard a loud noise outside. The wind was fierce, and we looked out to see a funnel cloud headed our way.

All of the old timers knew about tornadoes, so when anyone built a house, they always built a storm cellar, which was a safe haven where you could go when a tornado was threatening. We had just built such a cellar at our new house.

I instantly grabbed Anna's arm and told Xavier Jr. to come quickly. We took some food and bedding and called our dog, Duke. Making haste, we entered the cellar where we always had emergency supplies such as a first aid kit, water, a lantern, and food. As I closed the lid to the cellar, I could see that the twister was headed our way and closing fast. I would guess that it was less than a mile away.

I lit the lantern and secured the latch on the door. Duke, our pet Labrador, began to whine, and he let out a yelp every once in a while. We started to pray for our safety and that God would spare our house and barn as well. The echo of the sounds above our heads caused more fear among us. We held on to each other in death-defying grips and prayed in silence to our God above. We could hear the thunder and felt the ground around us tremble. This twister was out there raising havoc and, from the stories we had heard, probably leaving death and destruction as well. The storm passed in a matter of minutes, and we were anxious to assess the damages and to see for ourselves just what all had happened to our peaceful farm. As I raised the door to the cellar, a beam of sunlight pierced my eyes. The sky was clear, sort of like God's promise of the rainbow.

As we looked out we could see that our barn had been flattened level with the ground. There were two dead horses lying close by. The house, however, was spared. We thanked God for the safety of our cellar and for protecting us through the storm. Many items outside were gone while some new things were added. Our house was going to need some serious repairs, and we would need to buy some more horses for farming. We also had to rebuild the barn.

I worked hard and saved my money, and soon I bought another place much closer to Mom and Dad. I repaired the house and built a nice new barn. Now it was time to get a new brother or sister for Xavier Jr.

On the following June, we had our new arrival, a sweet baby girl we called Josephine. She was so lovable and cuddly that I could not put her down. Anna and Xavier Jr. were thrilled, and Olga was like her big sister. She thought that Anna had the baby just for her. Mom held her every chance she had, and I could see that she wanted more children, but she was past the age where she could conceive. More babies would have been all right with Dad because he dearly loved children, and he would play with them for hours at a time.

CHAPTER XIV
XAVIER CONT'D
DAD COLLAPSES

Dad was out working in the fields, getting ready to plant wheat, and his brother Edward had come to help him. Dad had complained about not feeling well at breakfast, and after a few hours, he collapsed on the seat of his tractor. Uncle Edward took him to the doctor right away, but by the time they got there, Dad was not breathing. The doctor tried to revive him for over thirty minutes, but it was no use. He said that Dad had suffered a massive heart attack that took his life. There was nothing that could have been done to save him. We all grieved for weeks and weeks, but what could we do? Dad had been there for us when we needed him, and we could always depend on him for good sound advice. Each of us dealt with Dad's death in a different way. Of course, Mom was devastated and felt the loss most of all. We would all spend time with her just knowing that she needed our love and support during these difficult days. Everybody agreed to help Mom with the work around the farm, and Michael would send his love and money quite often from Spain.

Dad had left his mark everywhere he went, especially on his family. We were survivors, but only because of Dad's teachings and the examples that he set for us to follow. He knew that this day would come, and he wanted to make sure that we were ready to take over.

FINDING DAD'S OLD LOVE LETTERS

It was weeks after Dad's heart attack that took his life, and I was helping Mom clean out the attic. There I found several boxes of miscellaneous articles of little or no value that had been stored there for many years. I noticed a small metal box that was locked, and it had a tag tied to the handle, which read: Open upon my death, Simon L. Roth.

I tried to open the metal box, but it had a hasp and a padlock securing its contents. I surmised that the key had long since been lost or misplaced, and so I tried to pry it open with no success. After several blows with a hammer, I broke the lock, and I was able to get it open.

The contents were a few old letters and some photos of people I didn't know. I was ready to discard them all when I found a sealed envelope that had the same message on it as the tag on the box: Open upon my death, Simon Roth.

I opened the envelope and found a picture of a young man holding a baby. After further inspection, I determined that the young man was indeed my father when he was very young. The child he was holding was not me or one of my brothers but did resemble Dad. The letter inside was dated several months after the end of the Franco-Prussian War:

August 27, 1871

My Dearest Simon,

I'm sending you a photo of us together with our son James at ten months old, taken at Mom's house here in Berlin. I pray every day for your safe and speedy return from this terrible war. May God bless you, especially while you are far away, and remember I will always love you.

All my love,
Frieda

SEARCHING FOR OUR LOST BROTHER JAMES

Who is this Frieda, this woman who claims to be Dad's wife? I asked myself. Is there some dark secret that Dad had not revealed to us? I wondered where Frieda and the boy were at this time.

After returning the letter to its envelope, I started to look for more clues to help me solve this perplexing problem. As I continued to examine the letters, I saw several letters that had been stamped, Return to Sender. These unopened letters were addressed to Frieda with Dad's return address. I hurriedly opened one of the letters:

My Darling Frieda,

It has been too long since your last letter to me, and I am very worried. Are you all right? I pray that nothing drastic has happened to you or to the boy. I'll be coming home in six or seven weeks for good as I will be getting discharged from the army at that time. I can hardly wait.

Much Love,
Simon

There were ten more such letters, each one dated about four days apart and each one essentially the same. Then I found another letter much more worn and faint, this one was rather difficult to read. It was from Helmut Becker, 1701 Milenburg Stassen, Berlin, Germany.

I was very curious as to whom Helmut Becker was and if he played a major role in this dark secret of Dad's. As I begin to read the letter, I could comprehend the whole story, and I began to choke. It must have been devastating news for Dad. The letter read,

Dear Simon,

You are like a brother to me, and it grieves me deeply to inform you that your darling wife, my sweet sister Frieda, has died of pneumonia. James, your son, is being cared for by Mom, Carmen Becker, whom you know to be a warm and loving grandmother to your son. She will contact you soon and tell you more.

Helmut

I saw another letter that Dad had addressed to Helmut. This letter was also returned to Dad unopened.

Dear Friend Helmut,

Thank you for your kindness and for advising me that my loving wife has passed away. It has been nine weeks since I received your letter but still no word from Carmen. My heart is heavy with this terrible loss.

I have been discharged from the army now, and I have gone to Berlin to find Carmen and my son, but they seem to have vanished.

No one has seen them or heard from them in the last two months. I left word with all the neighbors of my whereabouts and how to reach me, but I've never heard from anyone.

I'm hoping that you can help me find your mother so I can have my boy with me now that I am no longer in the army. I spent nearly a month trying to locate them, or you for that matter, but all I found was an old note that said she would be back in four or five days. The note was dated, August 28, 1871, only eleven days after Frieda's last letter to me.

Please help me in these my darkest days.

Sincerely,
Simon Roth

I did not tell anyone about the letter box and its contents. I was planning to divulge this secret after I finished my search to locate James, our brother, son of Simon. I spent about thirty days checking for his name in and around the Berlin area, but I had no success.

I was considering my options when the thought occurred to me that maybe he had immigrated to America like we did. Then I remembered that Ellis Island keeps excellent records of all immigrants entering the United States from Europe as well as many other places.

I wrote to them instantly, hoping to uncover some information about James. I gave them all the pertinent information that I could find. I had almost given up when I saw the mailman headed our way.

He hollered out, "Xavier, ya gotta letter from New York!"

CHAPTER XV
XAVIER
LOCATED LOST BROTHER JAMES

I opened the letter from Immigration with trembling hands:

Dear Mr. Xavier Roth,

> I received your letter requesting help locating your missing brother. After checking our records, I find James Simon Roth:
> Date of birth: 10-17-1871
> Mother: Frieda Roth
> Father: Simon L. Roth
> Immigration Date: 12-25-1899
> Arrived: on the SS Guggenheim,
> Port of Entry: Ellis Island, New York, N. Y.
> Destination: Minneapolis, Minnesota.
> I trust this will be of significant value in your search.

Sincerely,
Leonard Perez,
U.S. Dept. of Immigration

My head was churning, and I was in shock. Dad and James had come to the United States on the same ship on the exact same date. As incredible as it was, the facts upheld the story.

Of course there were over twenty-five-hundred passengers who had traveled on that ship, and no one had the passenger manifest except for Immigration and the captain. There was no way Dad could have known. I was sure I had found our oldest brother James, Dad's oldest son whom he hardly knew. I decided to wait until I contacted him before telling anyone.

I sent a letter to the Immigration and Naturalization Service in Minneapolis and explained the situation, but they could not give me his address even though they had it on record. They told me that if I would give them permission in writing, they would contact James and give him my address and a copy of my letter. James had a temporary residence card and was required to check in with the Immigration and Naturalization Service every six months until he received his United States citizenship. I was shaking all over, thinking that Dad would be so happy that his sons had finally met each other. I wished Dad could have known that James and he were on the same ship coming from Europe to the USA.

I felt bad as Dad was gone now without ever finding his lost son. How tragic that was, and how sad it made me feel!

Then a thought occurred to me. *Did Carmen purposely steal the baby from my dad?* Of course, that's the only answer. After all, Helmut did not accept Dad's last letter either, and he knew how to get in touch with Dad. I suspected it was a conspiracy as Helmut would side with his mother if she asked him.

I'll really never know the particulars of this incredible conspiracy until I asked James in person, "Just who raised you and what were you told?"

CORRESPONDING WITH JAMES

I quickly sent a letter giving permission to the Immigration and Naturalization Service in Minneapolis and a brief letter of explanation to James:

Dear James,

This will come as a shock to you, but I know without a doubt that you are my brother. Your father, Simon Roth, was also my father. He was called home to be with God only six months ago. I'm so very sorry!

You have two other brothers and a little sister, along with Simon's second wife, my mother, who also lives here with us in Aberdeen, South Dakota. It's only a ten-hour train ride from you there in Minneapolis to our home, so we are almost neighbors. I am excited beyond all imagination, and I still can't believe that I've found you after all the difficulty I have encountered. I learned of you by accident, which I will explain later.

The Immigration and Naturalization Service would not give me your address, but they have agreed to forward this letter to you. I do thank them for that. You can contact me at R. R. #1, Box 342, Aberdeen,
South Dakota, and I pray you will.

With much love,
Brother, Xavier Roth

PS: I can't wait to meet you, and I probably won't sleep until I get a reply from you.

I found myself on edge daily, waiting for the reply from James. I was sure that he was an honorable man, being the son of Simon, a man with compassion for all. I had been counting the days, and then the weeks, and finally, on the third week I checked the mail, and there I found a letter from James Roth. My excitement soared as I opened it:

Hello Brother Xavier,

I am absolutely thrilled out of my mind to know that I have a brother like you and two more brothers and a little sister. I am insane with emotions running wild.

I was told that my mother died when I was very little and that my dad was killed in the war. My grandmother raised me, treated me kindly, and provided for me.

I am so happy that you located me although it must have been difficult. This whole story is so unimaginable and intriguing. Our father, Simon, must have been a very special man, and I'm sure you miss him every day.

I can't wait to meet everyone in my new family. It's so incredible, and I have a thousand questions, as you must have as well. When can we get together?

It takes about ten or eleven hours by train to your house, so that shouldn't be a problem. My kids are eager to meet everyone and to ride the train. We are teachers at the college here in Minneapolis, but we met in Frankfurt, Germany.

We get three months off starting June 7, so we can go there to see you, or you can come here, whichever you choose.

I would imagine that you are married like myself and have children as well. Kathy and I have a boy, Jonathan, eight years old, and a girl, Estelle, who is six. They have asked me countless questions about all of you, for which I have no answers. I can only guess that we have much in common and have many of the same characteristics.

If you have any photos of Dad or any of our family, I'd love to see them. Possibly, you could write me a letter soon and include some pictures and more information about Dad and all of you.

I'm wondering if Simon was quite tall as I am nearly six-foot, six-inches tall, with blonde hair and blue eyes. Does this relate to you or to any of our brothers or to Dad?

I'm a music teacher, and I play many musical instruments; piano, accordion, and violin are my best I would say. Did Dad play music or do any of my brothers play? Could you tell me where I got my musical talent?

If you don't mind, I'd like to know some of the particulars about my family. The sooner I can find out, the sooner I'll be able to get some sleep. I'm very anxious to meet you and the rest of your family as soon as possible and at your earliest convenience, naturally. My entire family is excited beyond description, and they won't rest until we finally meet you all.

My grandmother was good to me, but she knew all the time that Dad was alive and just how and where to find him. I can't forgive her for misleading me. She made absolutely no effort, not even a mention of the truth when she was sick and dying. That's been fourteen years ago; why would she withhold the truth on her deathbed?

I know we can't make up these years that were stolen from us and forget what's happened. However, I do know that if I'm ever going to forget and forgive what my grandmother did, I need to somehow wipe the slate clean and make the best of the future.

You've shown that you are the kind of brother to help me take the first step, and now I'll do my part to show my appreciation for what you've done. I'm sure that's what Simon would have wanted, and I know that you will agree.

You will remain on my mind constantly and in my thoughts and prayers. I will try to be patient while awaiting your reply, but

I'm consumed with anticipation. I know how exciting this is for everyone concerned; please believe me. I anxiously await your reply.

PS: Xavier, I thank you again for your undying eorts; you really are a very special brother.

Love
From Minneapolis
Brother James and Family

As I absorbed the kind and meaningful words from James's letter, I became filled with pride of my wonderful family. Now we have another brother and his family with whom to share our lives. James and I seem to have really connected with each other. I couldn't wait to meet this big brother that I'd never met or have never known existed.

I gathered several photos that I thought would be of interest to James and his family. I decided to keep the picture of Dad holding James at ten months old and show it to him after he digests the others, sort of like a dessert, I guess.

I picked up a pen and paper and started to compose a letter to James. I thought about the days of my youth when my brothers and I would spend all day with Dad, just enjoying each other and learning new exciting things from him. I couldn't help but feel sorry for James because he had missed out on all that, and now he would never have a chance to know his father. What a tragedy! I would do the right thing; that's what Dad would want, and that of course would be to treat James like he was always a part of our family. My letter to James would reflect those feelings of acceptance and love:

Dear Brother James,

It's so inconceivable to know that I have a brother living close by that I have never met. I wish Dad had lived long enough to be reunited with you; he would have been so thrilled. I promise that I will do my best to welcome you into your late father's family. Your family is going to be a new and wonderful addition to my life from this day on while my family will be a part of yours as well. I'm sure you agree.

I'm so anxious to meet you, spend some time with you, and get to know everyone in your family. I imagine that you share the same feelings and know exactly how I feel.

I have enclosed some photos, as you requested, so you can get an idea of what to expect. Let me know what you think of your new family; is there any resemblance? Oh no, the one wearing the saddle is not Uncle Herman, it's Dad's horse, Blackie. He's not a part of the family anymore, but Dad had him for over twenty-one years.

I am open to whatever you decide for our reunion, and I agree it should be very soon. I live close to Mom and your young sister, Olga. Together we have room for many guests, at least ten or twelve. We are ready now, so let me know when and where to meet you.

You asked if Dad were tall. Yes, he was six-foot-five-inches, and my brothers and I are all six-foot-six-inches tall or slightly taller. Dad had blonde hair and blue eyes while my brothers and I are like Mom, with brown hair and gray eyes.

Please let me know your decision, and we will be ready. It's going to be more exciting than either of us could ever imagine. I can't wait to hear from you.

Much Love,
Brother Xavier
PS: Send a telegram reply if you can; I can't wait.

James's telegram arrived soon after:
WESTERN UNION
To Xavier Roth

Dear Xavier,

I'm in receipt of your letter. Stop. We are anxious to see you. Stop. We plan to arrive in Aberdeen on June 7, at 7:10 a.m. Stop. We are very grateful for your offer to house us. Stop. See you in a week. Stop.

Love,
Brother James

As I read these few lines, I knew my life was about to change forever, and somehow I knew that James was having similar feelings. I felt very close to this brother. Although we had never met, we were not strangers, for he was my brother, my father's son.

Now it was necessary to take the letters to Mother and show her what I had found. It was difficult at first, and when she read the letters, she was shocked. Dad had never told her of his wife, Frieda, or the son they had together. She remembered that Dad had accidentally called her Frieda two or three times when they first got married, but she had thought nothing of it.

When I told her I had been in contact with James, she was excited and told me that I had done the right thing. Then I showed her the telegram from James.

After she read it, she said, "Of course, he is welcome in my home.

After all he is Simon's own flesh and blood."

I thanked her for her understanding in the matter and reassured her that I would handle everything. I continued to prepare for June 7 and the 7:10 a.m. train from Minneapolis.

Next, I went to visit my brother Lambert to tell him the good news. As I reached Lambert's house, I could see he was holding his oldest son who had just fallen down and was crying. Magdalena was waving at me from the kitchen window with her usual big smile.

I called out, "Lambert, I've got some good news." He quickly responded, "What is it?"

I opened the box of letters that Dad had saved and told him that I had found them in the attic. I showed him the letter and the photo from Frieda to Dad.

He replied, "I don't believe it. Dad was married before Mom?"

"Yes, and I've located the boy in the picture. His name is James, and he lives in Minneapolis with his wife and two children."

Lambert kept shaking his head in disbelief as he continued to look at the photo of Dad and the boy.

I said emphatically, "We have a brother, Dad's oldest son."

Then I told him that James would be here in a week. He was still shaking his head as I rode out to go home.

When I got home, Anna asked me, "Who sent you the telegram today?" "My brother sent it."

She assumed that Michael had sent it from Spain and asked, "How is Michael doing? Is everything all right?"

"No, it's not from Michael."

Anna glanced up at me with a puzzled expression and blinked her eyes.

I could tell she was waiting for an explanation, so I continued, "Remember the letters I've been writing and the ones that came in the mail? I have a long-lost brother, a son of my dad's from a former marriage."

"Where are they now?"

"His wife died when the boy was only one-year-old, and the boy's grandmother stole him away while Dad was in the army. Dad tried, but he could never find them."

And so I relaxed and sat down to have supper with my family. After a few minutes, I smiled at Anna, and I asked her,

"How would you like to have company soon?" "Do they live here in South Dakota?"

"No, but they are coming on the train." "When will they be here?" "Next Saturday."

Anna smiled, walked over to me, and put her arms around me. She kissed my cheek and softly said, "Xavier, this is a miracle. It is so fantastic! I'm really happy for you all."

The week went by quickly, and soon we were at the train station waiting for James and his family to arrive. I heard the whistle, and then the 7:10 pulled up and stopped.

CHAPTER XVI
XAVIER
JAMES VISITS SOUTH DAKOTA

I was extremely nervous just wondering how James would accept us all. My heart was pounding, and I felt a bit dizzy.

We were all there to meet the train. Lambert and I stepped forward, looking for James to disembark. At that instant, he stepped from the train, and there was little doubt that our brother had arrived. We stood there, eye to eye, and it was such a special moment for everyone. "James Roth?" I eagerly asked as I reached out to embrace him.

"What a tremendous pleasure to meet you after all these years." "Xavier, Xavier, finally we meet. It's such a thrill!" I introduced

Lambert first, and they embraced. Lambert said, "Welcome, brother." James replied, "Thank you, brother."

I then introduced James to more of the family.

"This is my mother, Ingrid. Mom, this is James, Simon's oldest son, and James, this is our sister, Helen.

We call her Olga."

James hugged Mom and Olga and commented,

"Wow! I have a mother at last, and a little sister too. How absolutely wonderful!"

Olga smiled and offered a big greeting, "Welcome, Brother James."

Mom needed no push; she immediately held out her arms to receive James. "You are the image of your father. There's no mistaking that."

James introduced his wife, Kathleen, and his children, and Lambert did the same, then I showed off my pretty little Anna and our children. We had brought two wagons, and we soon set out for the farm.

It only took thirty minutes to make the trip home, so we stopped to invite Uncle Edward, Dad's youngest brother, to our house for lunch. He agreed to come to the house to meet James and his family and to have lunch with us even though he was working.

We had only been home about ten minutes when Edward and his family arrived. I had never seen anyone so excited before; James hugged everyone and asked many questions. Edward said he was five years younger than Simon and that he had known about Simon's wife, Frieda, and the son that Simon couldn't find. Dad had told him to keep it a secret, and Ed agreed.

Ed said that he had never met Frieda or the boy, but knew that Frieda's mother had stolen the boy away and disappeared, causing much heartache and devastation to Simon.

"I wish Simon could have met you, James. You remind me so much of your father," Mom continued.

"Now we have another wonderful young man and his family with whom to share our lives."

Mom and Anna had prepared some delicious food for lunch, and soon we were all gathered 'round the table. We talked as we ate. Mom asked James, "Where did you grow up as a boy?"

He replied, "In Southwest Germany, near Heidelberg." I interrupted and spoke directly to Mom.

"It's a long and complicated story, Mother. If you don't mind, I'll fill you in later."

Mom smiled and replied, "Of course, Xavier." "James," Uncle Ed said as he was leaving.

"It has been such a pleasure to meet you and your family. Sarah and I must go now, but I want to invite you all to our place on Sunday after church. We have several saddle horses and a lake where we can fish and swim."

We all anxiously agreed, and Uncle Ed replied, "Okay, we'll see you Sunday about 12:30." As they were leaving, James turned and said, "Uncle Ed is really a great guy." We all agreed.

We talked for hours, and Anna fixed a nice roast beef dinner with many other fine dishes. She asked, "Why don't we show the children where they are sleeping, just in case they want to go to bed?"

Anna took care of the children while the rest of us relaxed and continued our getting-acquainted conversations. Mom and Olga decided to spend the night at my place. Life was very good once again, and I thanked God for reuniting our family. I could see that James was about to fall asleep, so I suggested that we continue in the morning.

The next morning, I was up early to take care of my chores before anyone awoke. I wanted to be there when James came down the stairs so I could greet him good morning. Back in the house, I prepared coffee for James and me. I placed the photo of Dad holding James at ten months old beside his cup.

James was the first one downstairs, and he quickly greeted me, "Good morning, Xavier! Is this coffee for me?"

"Good morning, James. Yes, I hope you like strong coffee."

As he sat down, he spotted the picture that I had placed beside his cup. "Who's this in the picture?"

But before I could reply, he said, "Oh my, this is Simon and me, I believe, and that's my mother, Frieda. I've seen many photos of her over the years, but I've never seen one of Simon and me together before."

He was smiling as he spoke, and he looked up at me.

"Now I know there's no disputing the fact that Simon is my dad. We could pass for twins at age twenty-two."

As I looked at James, I saw a reflection of my brothers and myself. He was overcome with emotion, and tears were visible in his eyes. He tried to speak, but his voice was shaky.

Then he cleared his throat and tried again. "Damn my grandmother."

The children were still in bed, so James, Anna, and I were the only ones to witness this.

"May she rot in hell for her unforgivable sins. I was abducted by her and taken from my father only days before he came to get me. I could have known my dad, all of you, and your wonderful mother all of these years, if she hadn't been so selfish."

BONDING WITH JAMES

I leaned over to where he sat and placed my hand on his shoulder. He reached up and placed his hand on top of mine. He said no more, but the tears continued to trickle down his cheeks as he fought off his inward pain.

My brother James and I had just bonded in a mutual feeling of love and respect for our dad and for each other. We understood the pain and anxiety each other felt at that moment, and from that day on, we would always be there for each other. I asked, "Would you like to keep the photo?"

"Yes, if it's okay?"

Just then Kathleen came down stairs to where James and I were sitting. I held out the picture of Dad and him and said, "This is a picture of James and our father, when James was one-year-old."

Kathleen took the picture, looked at it, and exclaimed, "I know him!" James replied, "My dear, that is impossible, neither of us has met my father."

She insisted, "Yes, I'm sure of it. I met him on the ship when Jonathan was lost. He told me that he was Mr. Roth, and we talked."

James replied, "You know, I do believe you, Kathleen, because Immigration said that Dad and his family were on the same ship as we were, but we had no way of knowing."

Mom excitedly exclaimed, "Do you mean that Simon actually met Kathleen and Jonathon on the ship and did not know who they were?" We talked with sadness and remorse.

Anna brought us some biscuits and gravy for breakfast. I asked James if he knew that Dad was a musician. He said that he wondered where he got his musical talent. I asked him to wait a minute as I had something to show him.

"Of course," he quickly agreed.

I went to the closet in the hallway and came back with a very large case. I sat it down in front of James, and I could tell he knew what was inside.

I offered, "Open it, if you'd like."

His eyes lit up as he reached for the snaps that held the case closed. As he opened it, I could see he was surprised at such a beautiful and expensive accordion.

"This was Dad's, and he would play it by the hour while we all danced and sang. Play it if you want!"

He smiled, put the strap over his shoulder, and checked to see if he needed to adjust it. The strap fit perfectly. He continued to smile as he winked at me and started to play. He had a different style than Dad but was equally adept at playing. I was impressed with his wonderful talent and congratulated him. I told him that Dad would have been proud. He thanked me for the compliment and continued to play.

Soon the kitchen was filled with family, and everyone was enjoying the music. Mom peeked around the corner to see where the music was coming from. She came out in her robe and started dancing. We all laughed, and the kids joined in.

After James stopped playing, Mom asked if he would like to have Dad's old accordion. James just smiled and sat there in disbelief. Finally he said, "Anything that connects me to Simon is especially dear to me. I almost felt his presence when I was playing."

Mom agreed and added, "I know what you mean, James."

Then Mom asked me if I would object if she gave Dad's accordion to James as a keepsake of his father's.

"Mom," I said, "what a great idea! "Are you sure?" James responded.

"Your father would feel so good if he knew."

We all agreed, and it was settled. Simon's accordion would be Mom's gift to James.

GETTING ACQUAINTED

We spent some time over at Mom's place, and she gave James a few more mementos of his father. Mom showed James the house and barn that Simon had built and many of his projects that he was working on at the time of his death.

Sunday came very soon, and we found ourselves at Uncle Edward's. It was all so exciting. We took turns riding the horses while some of us went swimming in the lake and others caught fish. James and I took the boat out on the lake and just enjoyed the warm afternoon.

Soon, Aunt Sarah rang the dinner bell, and we all raced to the house. A picnic table loaded with tons of food awaited us, so we filled our plates and sat around in the backyard. The food was a typical South Dakota picnic, ending with homemade apple pie and some cold watermelon, which we quickly devoured.

The county fair had started, and Uncle Ed suggested that we spend the rest of the day there as it was only a fifteen-minute trip away. We spent much of our time riding the Ferris wheel and the other amusement rides, which were fun. We bought cotton candy, hot dogs, and peanuts. When it came time to go home, we almost had to drag the children away, especially Olga.

Back at Uncle Ed's farm, we had fun singing and dancing while Uncle Ed and James played their accordions. I could tell that they were having fun playing together for the first time.

It was getting late, so we thanked Edward and Sarah for the wonderful day, and we soon headed back to our place. We finally called it a day and retired early. It had been such a very long, eventful day, filled with joy and fun. Nevertheless, we were tired.

In the morning, Uncle Frederick who had been working in North Dakota stopped by to meet James and his family. He told James about his childhood with Dad and the different places they had lived when they were growing up. He was two years older than Dad and remembered Frieda and James as a baby.

FREDRICK REMINISCING

"I helped Simon look for you when he returned home from the war. We got very close one time as the innkeeper in Frankfort recognized the photos we showed him of Carmen and the baby. He said that she had been there just three days before, in the company of a younger man."

That turned out to be a dead end because there were many trains departing Frankfort in different directions, and we couldn't find her name on any of the passenger journals. She probably used a fictitious name from that point on to keep from being followed.

Simon was finally convinced that Carmon had taken James far away and was in hiding somewhere, but he could never determine where. He finally moved to Berlin where he met and married Ingrid Sorenstrom. They soon moved to Wiesbaden, where Simon farmed and was a blacksmith for years. He insisted that we keep all of this a secret as he was afraid Ingrid would be hurt knowing that he had been married before.

Uncle Fred had to leave and return to North Dakota to finish his job. He told everyone goodbye and gave James a big hug while wishing him continued happiness.

A short time later, James and his family had to return to Minneapolis, but we were now a genuine family; nobody could dispute that. Plans were made to go to Minneapolis in two months to visit James and his family and to see the big city.

Everything that had taken place was as if some greater power had willed it to be. These amazing events that had just unfolded were nearly inconceivable, but they actually did happen to our loving and devoted family. We had lost a father but had gained a brother and his family. From then on, we vowed to always thank God for guiding my path in locating James, our newly found brother.

As James's family boarded the train to leave, we knew that it was not goodbye; it was just the beginning of a new and wonderful friendship. We all waved and shed a few tears, knowing it would only be a few weeks until we journeyed to Minneapolis, to see them again.

Our brother James was not just an ordinary man he was a good father and a fine husband. He was a good musician and was extremely compassionate, always giving of himself and appreciating the wonders of life. He was very much like his father. Although James had almost no previous contact with Simon, he had his father's wonderful genes.

CHAPTER XVII
XAVIER
VISITING JAMES IN MINNEAPOLIS

After harvest, we all took the train to Minneapolis. James was able to obtain two extra bedrooms from a neighbor, so we could stay together while we were there. We took several short day trips to points of interest and were amazed at the size of this town. Aberdeen was less than 5 percent the size of Minneapolis, which included the university where James and Kathy were teachers.

James took us on a tour of the university, which was spectacular, as the campus was much larger than the whole town of Aberdeen. It was so beautiful.

He asked, "Do you want to attend a concert by my school's orchestra on Tuesday evening?"

We replied, "Yes, of course we do!"

We enjoyed this fine orchestra on Tuesday with James as conductor. Everyone was in agreement that it was spectacular.

"Kathleen wants to show you where she teaches chemistry and physics as she's extremely proud of her accomplishments."

"Yes, I'd like that," I replied.

We eagerly agreed and spent the rest of the afternoon with her. James had basketball practice and couldn't come with us, but we understood.

We continued on our tour of Minneapolis and could see that James and Kathleen were pleased that we had come to visit. James had many photos to share with us, and we got to see him at different ages throughout his growing years. It was especially fulfilling to share with him those early days of his youth.

He insisted that we take some of the photos, and I was hoping he would offer. They helped fill in the years between the photo of him and Dad and the man he was today.

He asked if we played sports at all, and I told him about my boxing career and of Michael's experiences in sports. He spoke of playing basketball and other sports. Right now, he was an assistant coach of the freshman basketball team, who was currently practicing despite being in the off-season.

We all decided to take a picnic lunch and go spend some time in the mountains. James took a fishing rod and caught a few rainbow trout. It was such a nice warm day that we all decided to go swimming in a quiet little lake, but we were told to be on the lookout for snakes.

Shortly, we heard a scream from one of the girls. We ran to see what had happened.

Estelle was holding her foot and was crying. "Dad, I've been bitten by a rattlesnake."

We were a long distance from any doctor, but I knew about snakebites from having lived in South Dakota. I quickly grabbed my pocketknife and cut a small X in each fang mark then I sucked out the venom and spit it out quickly. This continued for several more minutes. Then I ripped my shirt into long strips of cloth and tied a tourniquet around her ankle, which had already started to swell.

Everyone had made ready to depart for town, and we were soon at a local hospital. The doctor examined Estelle and immediately gave her a shot of anti venom and bandaged the area where I had removed the poison. He put on a new tourniquet and gave her some medicine. She was placed in a private room, and the doctor told us that the next few hours would be critical.

We all remained in the waiting room for over five hours until the doctor came out and told us that she was responding to the shot. He said that we could go in to see her now but only for a few minutes. He told me that I had saved her life with my quick actions.

The next morning Estelle was better, and we were able to take her home. She was sick to her stomach and had a headache for a couple of days, but soon she was fully recovered.

James made dinner for all with the trout that he had caught, and Kathy cooked some vegetables and rice. We all gathered around the table as James prayed, giving thanks to God for his child's recovery.

The time we spent with James and Kathy was special. We seemed to pick up right where we'd left off in South Dakota. It was sort of like we had known one another for years.

As we were leaving to go to the train station, I asked, "Can we expect you at Christmas?

James replied, "I'm agreeable to that. How about you, Kathy?"

"Yes, that would be quite nice."

As the train pulled away, I could feel a sort of sadness come over me again, like the last time we parted in Aberdeen. We had bonded in a powerful way, and I was drawn to James, who was so much like Dad.

We continued getting together at least twice a year, and I did enjoy my big brother enormously. We corresponded about once a month to make sure each other was all right.

CHAPTER XVIII
MICHAEL
MICHAEL INVITES MOM TO VISIT SPAIN

It had been two years since Dad had passed away, and Mom was pretty bored with life. Isabella and I sent her a card for her fifty-first birthday, on

April 28. In the envelope, I added a letter:

Dear Mom,

I miss you; we all miss you. Do you suppose that you and Olga could come over soon to visit us? We would like it so much if you could do that.

The children ask about you often, and Isabella is particularly fond of you. It would be so nice if you could come here and spend a month or two with us. Lisbon has ocean liners traveling direct to New York once every two weeks, and we would be happy to pay for all your expenses.

I was thinking that June or July would be a good time for your travel as the weather is decent and warm, and it takes less time than the trip through London. You would save nine days each way traveling. It's only about twenty- two days on the Atlantic Ocean, and you could bring anyone else that you'd like. We could meet you in Lisbon, and from there, it's only ten hours to our home.

The new and faster ocean liners are so comfortable, and they have excellent food and good music. Time goes by so fast, and you'll be here before you know it.

When you get here, we can go all over Spain or wherever you would like. Your sister Bianca could come from Germany and be our guest as well. We would be very happy to send her money for all of her travel expenses. It's only about four days from her house to Madrid by train, and the scenery is absolutely beautiful.

Since Olga doesn't start school for one more year, you can stay for as long as you'd like. We could have such a good time.

If this is of any interest to you, please send a telegram or letter quickly as we need to make plans. I look forward to your speedy reply; I can hardly wait to see you. It will be such fun if you can make it.

Love,
Michael

It was almost four weeks until I received a telegram reply from Mom. She was just like me, excited and filled with emotions. She was definitely agreeable to the idea and wanted to get started in a few weeks. Her telegram read:

Dear Michael,

Yes, Olga and I will come to see you. Stop. It would be so wonderful to see my sister Bianca as well. Stop. You have her address, so please get in touch with her right away. Stop. I'd like to leave South Dakota about June 10. Stop. Please take care of all my reservations and let me know when to be in New York. Stop. I can't wait! Stop.

Love, Mom

The reservations were made, and I sent Mom a telegram along with her itinerary. I also contacted Aunt Bianca again to advise her of her itinerary.

The ship was to leave New York on June 12 and arrive on the third day of July in Lisbon. I figured Isabella, Bianca, and I would all go to meet Mom and Olga. We could all have a grand time in Lisbon and on our travel back to Madrid.

The days went by quickly, and we soon found ourselves on our way to Lisbon. Mom would be there in about fifteen hours. Bianca had arrived in Madrid yesterday and was so excited that her loving sister was coming to visit. The last time they had been together was when Mom left Wiesbaden for Odessa, Russia, with us boys and Dad. That was over twelve years ago.

We arrived in Lisbon a few hours before the ship was due to dock, so we went to the Grand Lisbon Hotel first and checked into the Royal Garden suite. It was a formal garden suite with housekeeping facilities and adequate servant's quarters. I also reserved a Royal Suite for Mom and Bianca, which gave them two full-time maids at their command. We were tired after our long trip from Madrid; Mom and Olga would no doubt be the same.

As the ship moored, we could see Mom waving, and we were so happy that she had finally arrived. When she saw Bianca, she started to cry, and so did Bianca. As soon as Mom disembarked, they hugged and simply held on to one another for the longest time. Isabella was right there with her love and hugs.

I picked up Olga, who kissed my cheek and said, "Hello, Uncle Michael, we finally got here."

Then she told me about the trip on the big boat and about all the fun she had.

We soon arrived back at the Grand Lisbon Hotel and were escorted to our quarters. Mom was thrilled with the ornate, two-hundred-year- old hotel and the magnificent flowers that bloomed everywhere. We arrived at dinnertime, so we all went next door to the Toreador Club where Isabella was well-known.

After dinner, we gathered around for the floorshow to watch the fine entertainment. As usual, Isabella was invited to perform. She declined initially, but Mom pleaded.

"Please, Isabella, we've not seen you perform."

Isabella, who was always eager to perform, finally consented. There was a wonderful flamenco guitar group performing, and Isabella started to dance. The crowd was spellbound. After her dance routine, she sang a Spanish love song that brought her a standing ovation.

Needless to say, Mom was speechless. She gave Isabella a warm, loving hug and said, "You're wonderful, my dear, simply wonderful."

We retreated to our hotel where we all retired early. The next morning we were up at dawn and on our way to Madrid. After a very long uneventful day, we finally arrived at Isabella III, our wonderful home.

Mom was so excited when she saw our beautiful home.

"Michael, your home is so pretty, and Isabella, you are such a lucky girl to have this wonderful home."

We both thanked her and agreed with her, expressing our delight with our magnificent home.

The children were at their grandparent's home in town, where Mom, Bianca, and Olga were invited for dinner the next evening. I was wondering what Mom would say when she saw the palace where Isabella was born. I purposely did not brief Mom about Isabella's family, as I was awaiting Mom's reaction when she arrived.

The day was warm and beautiful, and our trip to town was exciting. "Isabella, have you always lived here in Madrid?" Mom inquired.

Isabella was at a loss for words, and so she just replied, "Yes, my love, I was born here, and I really love it so far."

Then Mother inquired as we pulled up in front of the palace, "Where is your parent's home?"

I interrupted, "Mom this is their home." "Why, it's a palace!"

"Yes, Mom," I added. "Her father is the King of Spain, and this is their home."

"The king, did you say the king?"

"Yes," Isabella replied. "He is a wonderful father and grandpa to your grandchildren. You'll meet him very soon. His name is King Alfonso."

At that moment, we pulled up to the main entrance. The children ran up to the carriage and hollered, "Grandma, Grandma!"

Mom held out her arms, and she hugged and kissed them saying, "My, but you children have grown so much." Mom introduced them to her sister, Bianca.

"This is my granddaughter, Heidi, and this is my grandson, Nick. Children, this is my sister who lives in Germany. Her name is Aunt Bianca."

Mom spoke German to the children as they were fluent in Spanish, German, and English.

"Hello," they politely replied.

"Won't you please come in so you can meet my mom and dad?" Isabella asked.

"Yes, I'd like that," Mom replied.

As we entered the palace, Isabella's mother greeted us with open arms. *"Bienvenido! Hola, todo."* (Welcome! Hello, all.) Isabella translated for her guests, but we knew that her mother was happy to see us as she quickly gave everyone a big hug.

About then, Isabella's dad entered the room. He was really happy to meet Mom and Bianca, and he was also very charming.

Isabella introduced them to us, and he gave us the traditional cheek-to-cheek greeting.

Isabella asked if we would like a glass of wine. Mom agreed, and we sat in the parlor while a servant brought in the wine. We all drank to our good health and just relaxed while Isabella translated our conversations.

Mom kept looking around at all the fine furnishings in disbelief. I'm sure she was as overwhelmed as I was when I first came here.

Isabella asked if we'd like to see the garden. "Yes, that would be nice," Mom replied.

We all followed as Isabella guided us through this splendid garden filled with many beautiful flowers, statues, and a sparkling fishpond. Mom was impressed with the roses, and she continued smelling them at every chance she had.

DINNER WITH THE KING

Soon it was time for dinner with the king. We all gathered in the formal dining room, and the fiesta began. I didn't know the name of some of the dishes that we were served, but I did know that they were delicious. It was a seven-course meal and so very well prepared. It took about two hours to fully enjoy such a wonderful dinner. We were all stuffed and couldn't hold another bite.

Mom and Bianca gave compliments about the fabulous food while everyone thoroughly enjoyed themselves. Soon it was time to go back to our house, and we reluctantly told everyone good night.

MOM'S VISIT TO SPAIN

The morning brought excitement and a bright sunny day, and we had big plans for a tour of the countryside. We also planned to take in the beautiful capitol city of Madrid. As we left the house, Isabella told Mom and Bianca our itinerary for the day.

Mom said, "That's a lot for one day. Can we do all that and still get home by dark?"

"Maybe we will not come back tonight. Perhaps we will remain in town, if that's okay with everyone!" Isabella replied.

I smiled and speculated that Isabella had a surprise for everyone. In fact, the day was extremely fascinating for Mom and Bianca with one surprise after another.

We stopped at the vineyard first. Mom and Bianca both loved the cellar where the wine tasting took place. Mom's favorite was the champagne, which was more than twenty years old. Bianca seemed to like it all but was especially impressed with the Vin Rosě.

Soon we were off to Madrid, where we had lunch at the oldest dwelling in the city, La Paloma. The place was packed, but Isabella was well-known by the owners. A table reserved for special guests only was made available immediately.

The entertainment was nonstop and the food surpassed all that one's imagination could afford. The wild game plate from the black forest, with five different meats and numerous other delightful foods was unlike anything I had ever tasted. We spent half the afternoon captivated by it all and finally had to force ourselves to leave.

Next, we headed for Chinatown, a traditional Chinese section of Madrid. The children loved it there and wanted to buy all the trinkets and puzzles they found. Mom bought silk pajamas for Olga and some presents for the grandchildren in South Dakota as well as something for James and his family. Isabella and I graciously paid for it all, but it was very inexpensive.

And finally, the surprise of the day! As we were leaving Chinatown, Isabella quickly guided us onto a huge, decorated, horse-drawn float. It was completely covered with flowers in the shape of a giant dragon. As we were about to relax, the king and queen of Spain were escorted onto the float and seated in the very front.

There was music everywhere, and there were many other floats depicting Chinese art. What's going on here? I asked myself.

It turned out that it was a Chinese holiday, and thousands of local Chinese were celebrating. There was a large parade with fireworks and cannons. The king and his family were being honored. This was why Isabella brought us to Chinatown early so we could be on the float when the parade started.

Isabella's father was Grand Marshal, of course, which was all so very exciting. We traveled through the streets of Chinatown with thousands of onlookers waving to us as we waved back. This was such a delightful time, and we were thrilled that it was held in our honor.

After the parade ended, we were seated in the beautiful Dragon's Breath Restaurant, which was located in the ornate Hong Kong Hotel. We were served delicious Chinese food, which surpassed one's imagination, and it was especially prepared for His Majesty and family. The floor show was so fantastic and colorful. The costumes were mostly lions and dragons, depicting the life and death of these fascinating people.

We were honored with a magnificent suite of rooms for the entire family, with all the complements included. Exotic flowers were present everywhere. We were delighted when breakfast was served in our rooms. The wonderful dishes were so very delicate and delicious.

The locals lavished endless gifts upon us for keepsakes and mementos. Mom got a silk, Chinese robe, and slippers while Bianca received the same. The children each got Chinese toys and colorful jackets made of silk. Isabella's mother was presented a sparkling diamond bracelet of twenty stones; each stone was about two carats in size, making it very beautiful and valuable.

The king received a set of engraved, gold-inlaid dueling swords from the Ming Dynasty era. They were museum quality and very rare. Isabella was presented a purebred Chinese dog called a Shar Pei while I received a hand-carved statue of a horse, believed to be very old, possibly three thousand years or more, and very collectable.

We graciously thanked them and departed for home. There wasn't much left of the day by the time we arrived home, so we sat about sharing our wonderful gifts and the memories of our Chinese experience.

The next day, Monday, we had not made plans for a trip anywhere, so we simply rested and made plans to visit the beach house in Valencia on Tuesday. We became even more excited as we were being told what to expect. We planned to spend at least two nights cruising on the royal yacht. The weather was slightly hot, so we knew that it would be somewhat cooler on the Mediterranean Sea.

We spent the first two days in Valencia playing in the sand and shopping in town. Mom and Bianca did not have any Spanish clothing at this point, and they needed something cool to wear. Isabella took them to her father's store and bought them many nice colorful outfits.

We all went back to Señor Arturo's, where Isabella and I had spent some time on our honeymoon. They loved Isabella's singing and dancing there, so again she accepted their invitation to perform. Soon she was wowing the customers with her talent extraordinary. Everyone wanted more, but she declined, choosing instead to shift the spotlight by introducing me, her husband, Prince Michael, and his family from America.

The next day we boarded the royal yacht and spent some time sailing around the nearby islands. We anchored each night at quaint fishing villages, taking in the local sites. It was so fantastic because everyone knew that the yacht belonged to the king, and we were treated with the utmost courtesy.

We spent one last night in Valencia before heading back to Madrid, just relaxing and enjoying the children in the wonderful pool.

When we got home, I asked Mom if she wanted to go to Bianca's house for a while before going home.

"I've enjoyed everything we've done, Michael, but let's save something for next time, if you don't mind."

Then came Sunday, and King Alfonso and his family usually attended church at St. Manuel's Cathedral, which was near the royal palace. We met at the eight-hundred-year-old church, which was strikingly beautiful and had been well maintained. The very ornate structure remained mostly original, with only a few small additions that were completed around the year 1790. The numerous arches gave the strength necessary to support the cathedral roof that had withstood centuries of storms and a countless number of wars.

After church, Isabella suggested that we go to Plaza Mayor, an ancient section of Madrid where shops and restaurants were plentiful. We found a popular spot named Margarita's for lunch. Isabella had gone there often since she was a child. The windows opened onto the streets, and the pedestrians strolled by. We enjoyed a special brunch called Huevos Madridiana, a delicious plate of eggs, potatoes, and scorched chilies with Black Forest ham and numerous local fruits and berries. There were also many pastries, and everything was extremely delicious.

We finished our food and were soon shopping in the many unique and unusual shops nearby. Most of the items were one-of-a-kind handcrafted works of art. There was artistic jewelry and many beautiful paintings prepared and crafted with extreme care. The rugs and tapestries and items of silver and gold were unique and gorgeous.

After buying many priceless items, we finally headed back to Isabella III, to watch the magnificent sunset. We relaxed and sipped on a very delicate Vin Rosě from our wine cellars.

The morning found us bound for Mueso Prado, a fantastic museum with ancient, Spanish artifacts dating back to four hundred BC. Such rare and priceless artistry that was quite unlike anything I'd ever seen. The paintings were especially breathtaking, mostly life-size portraits in gilded frames. We saw a painting of Isabella's great-great-great-great- grandmother at a very young age. Her name, of course, was also Isabella. There was a gigantic painting of her husband as well, King Ferdinand III, which was much like the painting in our bedroom; it was very old and valuable.

Our final day of touring in the Madrid area involved a trip to Toledo, an ancient city more than two-thousand years old that had been the Moorish capital of Spain. The city was built on a hill with a river on three sides, and it was virtually impossible to attack. It had withstood many wars until the Moors were driven out of Spain in 1492.

It was still maintained in its original style, with numerous historic sites and statues of great rulers from the past. We stopped to have dinner at Almeria's, a quaint pre-Columbian restaurant built by the Moors over five-hundred years earlier.

"Do you still have the delicious leg of lamb?" Isabella asked. The waiter responded, "Yes, it's our most popular meal."

Dining there felt much like going back in history to medieval times, an experience that I could never have imagined.

The next day we took Bianca to lunch, and then we bid adios to Mom's only sister as she boarded the train that would take her home to her family. She thanked Isabella for her wonderful hospitality and gave the children big hugs and kisses. With tears in her eyes, she bid us all farewell.

Though very pleased with the fun and excitement that we all had shared, Mom was soon ready to get started on her long voyage home.

"Now it is your turn to come and see us," she gestured as she let out a little smirk.

"I'll try my best to entertain you, but I doubt it will compare with all you've done for us."

I took Mom back to Lisbon to catch the ship, and we enjoyed just being by ourselves for the day while we traveled.

"I can see that you have a wonderful wife and family, Michael, and you are enjoying life to the fullest. Even though we are many miles apart, you are always in my thoughts and prayers."

Soon she boarded the passenger ship, the SS *Christopher Columbus,* not knowing when or if we would meet again. Xavier met her at the train station in Aberdeen, and shortly she was home at her own humble little farm. It was not nearly as elegant as the palace of the king of Spain, but it was home, and Mom felt at peace there.

CHAPTER XIX
LAMBERT
BROTHERS INVITED TO SPAIN

Mom brought a letter to Xavier and me from Michael and Isabella, which was an invitation to come to Spain to visit:

To: Xavier and Lambert

Dear Brothers,

We have enjoyed having Mom here to visit. We should have invited Dad while he was alive, but no one could have foreseen his untimely passing at such a young age.

Isabella and I have been over to see you three times since we married, and we would be so happy if everyone could come here to Spain and spend some time with us. We would be pleased to cover all of your expenses and give you the grand tour of Isabella's homeland as well as a chance to meet her wonderful family.

I believe the best time to leave South Dakota would be in mid-April, which would allow you to return home in July, in time for your annual harvest. It takes about twenty-two days aboard ship to Lisbon and then about ten more hours overland to Madrid, where we live.

If you could spend about five weeks with us, it would be so fantastic. Mom can fill you in on the many places to go and the fun things we could do while you are here. It's so much fun for the children as well, and the time at the beach in Valencia is sure to be the highlight of your tour of Spain.

Please let me know what you think so we can arrange your itinerary and make all the necessary reservations for you. We are extremely excited at the thought of it all, and we hope you are as excited as well. You'll have so many wonderful memories to take home with you, which you won't regret for a minute.

I recommend that everyone learn some Spanish, as it will be useful here where nobody speaks English or German, that is, except for Isabella and her children.

Don't bring a lot of clothing as it's hot here most of the time. We will get everyone summer outfits from the local stores when you get here.

I believe the children will miss some school, but they can bring their studies along. They can learn so much here about geography and history as well as the customs and language of the local people.

Send a letter soon and tell me your thoughts. I can't wait to see you.

Love,
Michael

As I read this very exciting letter of invitation, I was filled with anticipation. What an experience that would be, far surpassing my wildest dreams! The children would love it as well.

I immediately took the letter to Xavier and his family, and he quickly related to Anna and the children that we would be going to Spain in about six months.

I told Mom what the letter said, but she already knew about it. "Yes, I agree that you should go to Spain. Enjoy yourselves and visit your brother Michael and his famous family. You will be the guest of the Royal Family of Spain, complements of the king."

Soon spring was upon us, and we were anxious to depart. Michael arranged for everything and sent our itinerary to us through the mail. We were scheduled to depart Aberdeen for New York City on April 17, 1908.

We were excited to get started on our trip, and soon we arrived at Grand Central Station. We were greeted by two large carriages on which our trunks and luggage were quickly loaded. Then we were transported on a shuttle, ordered by Princess Isabella, to the Portuguese Princess, an ocean liner.

Our boarding time was here at last, and soon everyone was comfortably situated on the deck and waving goodbye to those on shore. Before long, we checked into the VIP Executive Suites. Each suite contained three bedrooms and three bathrooms as well as two full-time servants with their own quarters.

We were lavishly cared for with twenty-four-hour service for anything we desired. The children enjoyed the entertainment and strolls on the deck. One night we were invited to eat at the Captain's Table, where everything was elegant and the food was the very best.

When we arrived in Lisbon, Michael and Isabella were there to greet us. We stayed the night at the Ambassador Hotel. Since we only had two hours of daylight remaining that day, it was just too late to travel any great distance.

In the early morning, we had a nice breakfast and a cup of very strong Portuguese coffee. The trip was uneventful and took a little over ten hours, which left us exhausted. We headed directly to Isabella III and had a light snack before going to bed.

Everyone loved Michael and Isabella's nice home and their lovely children. The next day we were invited to the royal castle to meet the king and queen. It was so pleasant there, and we were served an enormous lunch that was delicious.

The king was cordial and friendly, and we talked about many things. Michael told him that we were going to Valencia to spend some time at the beach. He warned us to be careful as there had been pirate attacks along the Mediterranean Coast with killings and looting. The pirates would attack from the sea, causing a great deal of consternation among the people of this region.

"One can't be too cautious when confronted with these lingering threats," he added.

We promised to take extra precautions and to carry a pistol. Isabella spoke politely to her father in Spanish, but I did not understand their conversation. She told us that the king had offered the royal guard to escort us, and it would be considered improper to refuse him. He had dealt with these unsavory renegades before and mentioned that he had several in his prisons at this time.

CHAPTER XX
MICHAEL
BROTHERS VISIT SPAIN

I had planned to take Lambert and Xavier on a tour of Spain, so we left Madrid and the families behind with the agreement to meet again in Valencia in two weeks.

We headed east to Barcelona on the Mediterranean Sea, stopping along the way to take in some bullfights as we continued to enjoy the scenic coastline and beaches. We were accompanied by the three royal guards furnished by the king, so we felt safe.

A ferry took us out to Mallorca where we spent some time in Palma, a beautiful seaport city of ancient Spain. We soon headed back to the mainland at Alicante Province, west of Valencia, where we spent the afternoon and the night along the Mediterranean waterfront. We just relaxed and enjoyed ourselves while reminiscing about our youth and those dreadful years in the Cossacks.

Soon we were on our way to Valencia to meet up with our families and sail about in the royal yacht. We arrived one day ahead of schedule, so we hung out at the beach house of the king. The next day we were anxious to get going, so we went to the royal yacht to get everything ready, telling the servants at the beach house to advise our wives where we had gone.

After getting the yacht ready to go and telling Captain Raul to stand by, we went out for lunch. The women and children were not there yet, but we were not really concerned.

BROTHERS CONFRONT PIRATES

As we returned from lunch, we noticed a great deal of commotion around the Royal Yacht. We could see numerous men with rifles and a Spanish galleon close to the yacht.

Shots rang out, and someone yelled, "Watch out, there's a pirate attack on the king's yacht!"

We immediately took cover to avoid any chance of getting shot. Just then, I noticed that the yacht's engine was running, and it was trying to get away. The naval ship closed in behind but was moving slowly. It was intentionally blocking the yacht from leaving its moorings.

The Spanish police had come to where we had taken cover. They pointed their rifles at us and yelled, "Put up your hands!"

Michael quickly told them who he was, and they in turn advised us of the situation. Our wives and children had just boarded the yacht when it was overpowered by the pirates. Our families were being held captive on board the king's yacht along with Raul, our skipper, and three mates.

This made for a very delicate situation. Xavier suggested that we get rifles and pistols from the naval ship for us three brothers. The weapons were immediately delivered as requested.

I noticed a ladder hanging over the stern that could be used to board the yacht without being detected, and I told Xavier. We spotted a small dinghy tied up close behind the yacht. Since it was almost dark, we decided to use it to make our move.

As we climbed the ladder to the aft deck, the naval vessel turned on their floodlights exposing the pirates on the fore deck and causing them to become nervous. They immediately fired shots trying to break the floodlights on the naval vessel.

This was exactly what we needed as everyone's attention was drawn to the front of the yacht. We quickly moved to the bridge where two pirates and their captain were trying to position the yacht in order to escape. A hand-to-hand fight ensued on the bridge, and soon we held the pirates under our control.

We demanded that the rest of the pirates surrender, or we would kill their captain. Many jumped ship into the harbor while the rest resisted. Shots were exchanged, and three pirates were killed. A glancing bullet hit me in the shoulder, but luckily Xavier was able to stop the bleeding. The navy was quick to board the yacht and disarm the few remaining pirates who had surrendered. We brothers held the captain and two pirates at gunpoint on the bridge. The pirates' plot had failed.

Our wives and children were happy to see us when we opened the door to the hold. Xavier bandaged my shoulder and found the wound to be only superficial, much to Isabella's relief.

We were surprised when Isabella's friend, the owner of Arturo's Restaurant, sent us a message:

Dear Princess Isabella,

I have observed your confrontation with the pirates from my front balcony, and I wish to console you and your family. Please come and dine with me as my guests in my personal quarters. It's private and quiet here.

Respectfully,
Arturo

We eagerly accepted and found the solitude most relaxing. After a quiet dinner, we went back to the royal beach house and just relaxed for the rest of the evening. I asked the captain of the guard to post some extra men at the house for continued protection.

We decided to spend a few more days just sailing around the area. Isabella requested a naval escort to guard against any further intervention by the pirates or any other faction.

AUTHOR
BROTHERS REWARDED BY KING

Word soon got around that Prince Michael, along with his two brothers, had overpowered the pirates and rescued Princess Isabella as well as many members of her family. They were acclaimed national heroes from every corner of the country for being brave and skillful warriors.

Isabella was thankful to Michael and his brothers for their vigilance and courage. The king soon became aware of this outstanding bravery in the rescue of his daughter and grandchildren. He awarded the Spanish Medal of Valor to the three brothers as well as the Naval Captain and honored them with a spectacular parade.

Once again, the three Roth brothers had proven themselves. Now the world knew just what these brothers were made of. Their Cossack training and fighting experience had proven, once again, to be invaluable. Prince Michael and the American Roth's were the hot topic of conversation throughout Spain for the coming weeks and justifiably so. The populace easily recognized them because they were nearly one foot taller than most other men on the street and because they proudly wore their Medals of Valor everywhere they went.

They were, without a doubt, in good favor with the king. He was well aware of their continuing and unyielding dedication to

Isabella. Their every wish was his command. A dinner was held in their honor at the palace, and all the family attended. The king personally granted Xavier and Lambert each one hundred acres of prime vineyards next to Isabella III. Their wines would be named, Xavier Valiente Vino and Lambert Valiente Vino, with all profits from these wines to be transferred to the brothers in the United States indefinitely.

MICHAEL

We were now ready to spend more time in Madrid. We decided to stay another two weeks enjoying the wonders of Spain and her fascinating people and taking in the many sights.

Izzy took us all back to Chinatown, where the children were fascinated beyond belief. We all loved the Chinese food and even took some home to Isabella III.

We toured Madrid and Plaza Mayor, where we had taken Mom when she was here. Everyone bought many nice crafts and some tapestry. I was happy to buy the souvenirs for them as I knew they had limited funds.

Again we went back to Toledo. It was not easy shopping there as we really needed a guide to find our way around. We asked around and were able to find a terrific local guide who was most helpful.

Everyone was fascinated with this ancient city which hadn't changed for over two-thousand years. There were no large buildings, only street shops and open-air markets. Donkeys and burros pulled carts up and down the streets, selling food and their wares.

Again, we had dinner at Almeria's, with many wonderful local dishes.

It was like going back to the days of Jesus, except for the language.

LAMBERT

We were out of time and had to go home in a few days. We thanked the king and queen for their hospitality and bid farewell to Isabella and Michael, thanking them for everything. We were soon aboard ship headed for home, with warm memories of Spain and our fascinating royal family.

CHAPTER XXI
XAVIER
BROTHERS RETURN HOME

It was nice to be home again, but it was almost harvest time, and there was much work to be done.

Mom was happy to see everyone, and we were happy to see her smiling face. Her wheat was nearly ready to harvest, so I made arrangements with the neighbor who always did this work for Mom.

She asked, "When is Michael coming to South Dakota again to visit?" I replied that he wanted to come the next time James would be here. "That should be at Christmas."

I advised her that the ocean was very stormy in the winter, so I needed to contact both brothers, suggesting that June would be a better time.

"That sounds good to me," Mom replied.

I explained to both Michael and James that June would be the best time to meet in Aberdeen, and everyone agreed to that date. Time flew by, and Michael was soon on his way. He was due to arrive on May 30 while James and family were coming on June 5. What a perfect time for such a momentous meeting!

JAMES MEETS MICHAEL

We went down town to the train station to greet Michael and his family. They were happy to be here after the long boat ride. We went straight to Mom's house where she had lunch ready. She was so happy to see everyone. We had six days before James and his family were due, so we helped Mom around her place, where work was always waiting to be done.

Once again, we all met the 7:10 from Minneapolis. This time Michael was there to greet James, whom he had never met. As the train came to a stop, Michael quickly checked everyone who disembarked. The rest of us stood back in the shadows, only observing, so as not to diminish in any way the drama and the thrill of this first meeting between these two brothers, both sons of Simon.

James was helping his wife and two children off the train when Michael spotted him. At that same time, James looked up to see Michael waving at them.

Both brothers ran with open arms to meet and embrace each other. Each one was extremely excited as we all converged on them with exuberant hugs.

"I see that you need very little introduction. James, meet Michael, and Michael, meet James. James, meet your beautiful sister-in-law, Princess Isabella of the Royal Family of Spain. Michael, meet Kathleen, the sweet and charming girl who has captured the very heart of your big brother James."

I added, "Welcome, children, meet your cousins."

Everyone exchanged hugs while James and Michael held onto each other long after the introductions. We gathered their luggage and departed for Mom's place. She was eager to see James and his family. She had prepared some wonderful food that everyone quickly devoured.

Prior to their meeting, I had briefed both Michael and James about each other's history and other important milestones in their lives. Nevertheless, they exchanged many polite inquiries and complements during their conversations, which helped acquaint them.

The children were already off by themselves having fun together, just as if they had always known one another. The camaraderie was amazing. Everyone's last name was Roth, and that seemed to be the standard of acceptance. Everyone was family!

Mom soon joined in to welcome all to her home and to the home of their grandfather who had built this house only a few years before. She bowed her head and prayed,

"We give thanks, O Lord, for your countless blessings and for uniting James and Michael. We ask for your continued blessings and guidance for this family in all we say and do, Amen."

Michael, not wanting to leave anyone out, asked James and his family to be their guests next summer in Spain. James committed for the visit to Spain, and Michael offered to take care of all the costs for the entire family. The date was set for a June 29 arrival in Lisbon, and everyone was excited.

LAMBERT

After spending some time in South Dakota, my family and I learned to love the friendly, prairie people. My wife Maggi eventually gave birth to four boys and three girls.

I was angry a lot and still unsettled from the curses of war. I couldn't find peace of mind or any peace with my darling wife, Maggi, which of course made me sad. Maggi came down with tuberculosis at the age of fifty-nine and died ten months later. Oh how I miss her! We all miss her big smile and loving ways.

I was not close to my children, except for Helen, my youngest, who lived at home with me until she was forty-eight years old.

She had no children of her own but was very happy with her husband Marvin while living in Nebraska in her later years.

AUTHOR

Xavier and Lambert continued to contract in the Dakota's and prospered. They enjoyed their lucrative royalties from their Spanish vineyards, and brothers James and Xavier were always in touch. The four brothers and Olga were blessed with many wonderful grandchildren and continued to enjoy each other.

Michael and Isabella came to visit South Dakota several times before Ingrid died. However, they loved living in Spain, with their two remarkable children. He and Isabella never left each other's side until the unfortunate day that Isabella was present when an assassin's bomb exploded on the front steps of the palace. The bomb that was intended for the king missed its mark, and Isabella and her mother were both killed instantly, leaving Michael and the children hopelessly grieving their deaths.

CHAPTER XXII
AUTHOR
SONJA'S STOPOVER IN VALENCIA

Devastated and dejected by personal tragedies, Sonja decided to take some time to travel. She was hoping to recover from her fragile, emotional condition. She soon found herself on a cruise down the Mediterranean Coast of Spain, enjoying some peace and quiet in a quest to settle her nerves.

Sonja began to reminisce about the romance that she had abandoned to become a nun, and now the memory of it all had returned to haunt her. Remembering that Michael had married Isabella, a girl she had once known in Berlin, Sonja recalled that they now lived in Spain. After contemplating a while, she decided to contact the Spanish Consulate in an effort to locate him.

When she gave them his name, they replied, "Do you mean Prince Michael?"

Sonja was surprised to learn that Michael had married a princess. She asked if she could have his address, and they gave her the address of the king's beach house in Valencia where Michael now made his home. She had planned to stop over in Valencia in just a few days. She debated, *Do I attempt to find him, or do I simply pass on by and not bother him?*

As Sonja arrived in Valencia, she noticed a special shop along the beach, The King's Beach Wear. After choosing some cool garments, she asked the clerk, "Does the king actually own this store?"

She was surprised when the clerk confirmed that he really did own the store. As they continued their conversation, the clerk casually mentioned that the princess and her mother had both been killed by an assassin's bomb on the steps of the palace only six months before. The clerk recounted that the bomb had been intended for the king, but fortunately, he was not injured.

"What about Prince Michael? Was he harmed?"

"No, he and the children were not with the princess at the time." "Does he ever come to the store?"

"No, but he lives close by and dines most every evening at Arturo's, next door."

Sonja was ecstatic just knowing that she had located Michael. Excitedly, she returned to her hotel to make ready for dinner at Arturo's later that evening.

As she reminisced, she thought about her last meeting with Michael. It seemed like only yesterday when they had spoken their fond last goodbyes, but she realized that had happened over twenty-two years prior. Remembering how extremely difficult it was to part, she recalled the thrill of that wonderful final kiss, a kiss destined to last an eternity. She also remembered their tender exchange of affectionate, loving words that time could never erase.

She gave much thought as to how he might feel about her now. Would he remember what they had once shared? Would he be happy to see her, or would he still be indisposed from the recent loss of his wife?

Sonja always prayed, especially when she was in need of guidance, and now she did just that. She was still very much in love with Michael and was holding on to those precious moments from the past, those moments that were concealed deep inside her heart.

As she approached the front door of Arturo's, her heart began to pound. The time was 8:45 p.m., and she supposed that most of the dinner patrons would be there by now. She stepped inside the dimly lit club and just stood there, quietly trying to focus her eyes.

The silence was soon broken when the maitre d' asked, "Dinner, madam?" Her eyes scanned around the smoke-filled room as she searched frantically for Michael's familiar face. She checked once more, but again she was unable to find him. She noticed a table for two in a quiet corner, and she nodded toward it and replied, "Yes, that table will be suitable."

As the maître d' politely seated her, she asked, "Is Michael Roth here tonight?"

"Not yet, but he should be arriving soon. Would you like me to give him a message, madam?"

"Yes, that would be splendid of you."

She quickly fumbled for a card in her handbag and gathered a few coins for a tip. Then, she added, "Ask him to join me if he pleases."

The music started at nine sharp, and her attention suddenly shifted from the front door to the stage. A lovely dancer appeared in the spotlight, noticeably glittering from the sparkles on the costume that she wore. To the delight of the crowd, she began a slow rendition of the Spanish Fandango, which escalated into an energetic, show-stopping performance.

Sonja didn't notice as Michael entered the club, but the maître d' was quick to hand him Sonja's card. He explained to Michael that "the lady requests the presence of your company, if you please, sir."

Michael strained his eyes as he tried to read the card in the dim light of the club. Dr. Sonja Girko was all he could make out as he was escorted to Sonja's table. Just as he was about to be seated, Sonja glanced up. Michael just stood there in shock with a look of disbelief.

MICHAEL
SONJA DINES WITH MICHAEL

"Sonja, Sonja my dear," Michael said as he held out his hands to greet her. "Is it really you? What brings you here to Spain, my dear?"

Sonja rose, and Michael kissed her cheek while they embraced with such tenderness that they attracted the attention of the entire room. They were both overcome with giant tears of emotion. Michael signaled for the waiter and requested a private room.

Michael, who was still in shock, began to ask the usual polite questions. "How are you doing, and how is life treating you?" "I'm quite well, thank you, and you, how are you?"

"Oh, I'm not doing well at all. The assassins murdered my darling wife and her mother six months ago, which diminished greatly my reason to live. I seem to be doing slightly better each day as I'm trying hard to be strong for my children. They are suffering terribly."

"I don't see your habit, Sister. Are you still in the Order of the Nuns?" Sonja replied, "I don't know where to begin, Michael. There's so much to tell. Do you remember Petrov, my one-time fiancé? I ran onto him about one year after I received my doctorate degree in Clinical Psychology. It so happened that I had a patient named Brasova Girko who was extremely psychotic. It turned out that she was Petrov's wife. "Brasova was a hopeless mental patient who was completely unable to function, and her prognosis was bleak. She escaped from her quarters one evening and jumped from the roof of the sanitarium, ending her life. I blamed myself for my failure to help her and resigned from the Order of the Nuns.

"Petrov and I became very good friends after all of this, and later we were married. He became ill about a year ago and passed away as a result of poor health and his war injuries. Then I was left alone.

"I decided to take a trip as I thought it would help with my fragile emotional condition. I soon ended up on the Mediterranean Coast, searching for some peace and quiet to settle my nerves. Then suddenly I found myself wondering about you, Michael, and recalling the romance I had abandoned to become a nun.

"I knew that you had married and had moved to Spain, but I didn't know exactly where you were. I did some checking yesterday, and I found that you were living here, in Valencia, at the king's beach house.

"Since Valencia was my next stop, I thought it might be nice to say hello. I had no idea that you too were single again, and I do hope that I'm not invading your privacy. Please tell me if I am, and I'll say goodbye this very moment."

Michael replied, "Absolutely not, Sonja, I'm delighted to see you again after all these years. You're even more beautiful now than ever before, if that's possible. I must admit that the timing could not be better for me, and I hope it is for you as well, my dear."

"Fate has brought us back together again, Michael, don't you agree? Just look at me. I'm sitting here across the table from you, Michael, my one and only true love and my dearest friend in the world."

"I hope you'll stay, Sonja. We both need each other now, more than ever before. I was never able to stop loving you all these years, and now I know why. I do believe that fate has determined that we should be together again, and I'll never let you go this time, no never, I promise."

"I believe that it is meant to be, Michael."

"You'll be pleased to know that I have two spectacular children, ages twenty and twenty-one. They are with me when they are not at the university. They miss their mother so much, and I would like them to meet you."

"Yes, Michael, I'd be honored to meet them. If they are anything like their father, they are sure to be wonderful."

CHAPTER XXIII
SERENDIPITY

Sonja and Michael spent nearly ten days getting reacquainted while relaxing at the King's Palace in Valencia. They were enjoying the ancient architecture and scenery along the Mediterranean Sea.

Michael's children were in college and later that day, would soon be home later that day for spring vacation for the surprise of their lives. Princess Isabella was horrified at being the first to enter her father's home, for it was there she discovered a strange woman residing with her father. Sonja was apologetic for her unannounced intrusion into Michael's home, which caused everything to go out of perception quickly. Princess Isabella was not accepting this new stranger whose role was to replace her recently murdered queen mother. She quickly stomps off to her room in what appeared to be an unacceptable rage, not to return that day.

The following day, they found the princess packed up and gone out of the house. This complicated the issue even more with clouds of uncertainty. There was no note or explanation left by the princess. Prince Charles had graduated from college and the whole family attended the ceremony except for Isabella, she was a "no show." Michael went to the university registration office, but the princess was no longer enrolled. After considerable effort, it was found that she had not attended school for the past ten months. The police were summoned, but no princess was found.

Sonja and Michael continued to live at the King's Summer Palace in Valencia, but there was no contact from Princess Isabella. Michael blamed himself for his failure in keeping track of his daughter, but she had broken all ties with her father and his new wife, Sonja. Meanwhile, Michael and Sonja lived at the palace. They continued to search for the princess, but she could not be found. Soon large boxes of fruit and vegetables were being left on their front step every morning. Not knowing where the food came from, they only accepted it as a gift from some loyal admirer.

Michael knew that the gardener was at work very early, so he asked him, "Who brings fruit and vegetables every morning?". The gardener replied only with "the village girl." No one knew just who this girl was, and could not identify her. Later when he was on the path to his house, he suddenly saw that she resembled his princess daughter and he called out her name.

The princess, knowing that she had been caught, rushed to her father with tears flowing and open arms and love in her heart, ready to come home at last. Everyone was hugging and happy that Isabella was finally home. Sonja and Isabella soon became friends to everyone's delight and Michael was once again at peace in his heart.

EPILOGUE

AUTHOR

War is hell. Even those who survive don't always recover from the psychological damage. The wounds of the mind don't always heal as quickly as those of the flesh. Sometimes people never heal from the sort of hell that war inflicts. One can only learn to cope as best as one can and deal with life as fate allows.

Yes, the battles were over for the three brothers who had returned from "The Living Hell." However, they were not the same boys that had been kidnapped from Odessa at gunpoint only a few years earlier. The trauma of battle had torn them apart. Even decades later, Grandpa remained a prisoner in his own mind, unable even to speak about many of the horrors that had changed his life from a peaceful farmer to an assassin of other humans. He could never let it go completely, regardless of how hard he tried. He was always asking for God's forgiveness.

At my grandfather's funeral, I found myself reminiscing about his life. My mind wandered back to the many tales he had told me of those years when he was a young man. The most memorable of all those tales was his accounting of his years in the Cossacks. I too could never forget those blood-curdling and unbelievable accounts of the hand-to-hand combat encounters that had been so vividly etched in my eager young mind. Those stories yielded so many sleepless nights and still seem to occupy my thoughts even today, more than seventy years later.

While I viewed his lifeless body, I could not help but remember his stories of so many near-death experiences, and his struggles to recover from those life-threatening injuries that he encountered. As I marveled over the massive frame of this fallen Goliath, I began to understand just how he was able to defy the adversities to which he had been so brutally subjected.

I can only say with unequivocal certainty that I am privileged to have his DNA flowing through my body, instilling the pride that I feel with each and every breath that I take.

Now when I look back at my grandfather Lambert, I see a picture of this stalwart giant. His face furrowed and hardened from the pain and agony of battle such that no man should ever be forced to endure. He'd been doomed to suffer a lifetime of torturous memories that completely deprived him of his emotional existence. Yet his courage and undaunted resolve remained unrivaled throughout his entire life.

The facts speak for themselves. Peace of mind is never easy to find for those who have been forced to kill or be killed.

AUTHOR'S NOTES

Now that I have finished this novel, I can look back at my accomplishments and feel good that I've kept my promise to my grandfather. I'm sure he would be happy to know that I've finished the book of his life's adventures and that I have been true to my word.

Writing about my ancestors has made me very proud of my heritage. These people were not just ordinary people; they were brave, kind, compassionate, and responsible humans. My heart is filled with pride as I relate these tales of intrigue and the touching dramas of their romances.

Their religious upbringing and faith in God was, in essence, the driving force that sustained them through the hell they were forced to endure. My grandfather's stories and the memoirs that he and his brothers have given me have provided me with these unbelievable adventures that I'm compelled to share with the world.

The word Cossack means "free adventurer," and my heart seems to have a longing to be just that.

SELECT BIBLIOGRAPHY

Carter, Miranda. George, *Nicholas and Wilhelm: Three Royal Cousins and the Road to World War I*

Radzinsky, Edvard. The Last Tsar: *"The Life and Death of Czar Nicholas II."* New York- Doubleday. 1992.

Specter, Michael. "Moscow Is Almost Certain Anastasia Died with her Czar Nicholas II Family."

The New York Times. September 7, 1994.

Ure, John. *The Cossacks: An Illustrated History.* Overlook Press. 2002.

PERSONAL INTERVIEWS

Roth, Helen, Great Aunt (Olga,) Interview, 1970.

Roth, Lambert, my grandfather. Interviews, 1936 to 1948, Adventures of his life.

Roth, Norman, my second cousin and grandson of Xavier. Interviews, 1968 to1979, Adventures of the brothers' lifetime.

www.ingramcontent.com/pod-product-compliance
Lightning Source LLC
LaVergne TN
LVHW091539060526
838200LV00036B/669